The Entir

Gregory Heath

WAYWISER

First published in 2006 by

THE WAYWISER PRESS

9 Woodstock Road, London N4 3ET, UK
P.O. Box 6205, Baltimore, MD 21206, USA
www.waywiser-press.com

Managing Editor
Philip Hoy

Associate Editors
Joseph Harrison   Clive Watkins   Greg Williamson

A CIP catalogue record for this book is available from the British Library

ISBN-10: 1-904130-21-6
ISBN-13: 978-1-904130-21-5

Printed and bound by
Cromwell Press Ltd., Trowbridge, Wiltshire

for Moy McCrory,
with thanks

At precisely ten o'clock every Sunday morning the front door of a terraced house in Alma Street opens and a man in a brown polyester suit emerges. He walks slowly down to the bottom of the street and makes his way through Woodington to the Anglican church on Wilne Lane. On a typical morning he'll pass a dozen other people and most of them will say hello. 'Hello, Dennis,' or, 'Hello, Mr Marshall.' You could be forgiven for thinking that everybody knows him, but it isn't true. He's been Michael's father for almost forty years and Michael doesn't know him at all.

A market gardener by trade, Dennis Marshall doesn't belong in a terraced house. He belongs back on Broadacres Farm, in the tiny hamlet of Wenleigh, a mile and a half out of the town. He was born in nearby Calke Valley, the best part of which now lies submerged beneath a billion tonnes of water. In 1956, when the valley was dammed and flooded to make the Staunton Harold Reservoir, he made the short journey to Broadacres, and spent the rest of his working life in the shadow of the dam wall. Now, a chronic lung disease and the lack of a son prepared to follow in his footsteps have brought him to Alma Street. And the death of his wife, a long time ago, takes him to the church.

When Nancy was still alive, Dennis was not a church-going man. He refused to attend, except for weddings, funerals and the harvest festival, and even then he was like a fish out of water. He wouldn't sing the hymns, he wouldn't recite the prayers. While the rest of the congregation did what was expected of them, he would stare blankly at his feet.

Michael would watch him out of the corner of his eye, and

wonder what he was thinking about. Michael still wonders. He wonders what his father thinks about now, now he goes to church of his own accord. He wonders: *Does he say the prayers now? Does he talk to her in his prayers? Does he believe she still exists, somewhere, out there, to be talked to?*

Michael's mum always believed. She had faith in God's love. And she must have had the same kind of faith in his father's love too, because Michael can't imagine Dennis ever putting it into words.

Did that bother her? he asks himself. *Was she, deep down, waiting to hear him say those words, or return from the fields one day with an unexpected bunch of wild flowers? Or did she know that it was too much to expect, that he couldn't speak the language of love?*

Or am I just excusing him? Couldn't he have picked her the flowers, for Christ's sake, and while he was at it couldn't he have given his sons the occasional pat on the head, the odd display of affection? Couldn't he have just given us something to start the ball rolling, some small beginning, so we could all have started to talk to each other before it was too late?

Because it is too late now. He can spend the rest of his life in that church trying to make it right, but it never will be.

A week before the baby was due, Dennis sent the boys to stay with his sister up in Edinburgh, where she ran a private nursing agency. Phil, the elder of the two, and always the one for a conventional response, thought it was a great idea. Michael can still remember the day they went; Phil was ecstatic, jumping up and down with excitement. Two weeks in Scotland, two weeks in another country! And to go on a train! They'd never been on a train before.

But Michael didn't want to go. While their father put their suitcases into the back of the Transit, ready to take them to the station, he sulked in the hallway. And when he came back in to collect the last case Michael made a last-ditch attempt to get out of the trip. 'But I don't like Aunt Eileen, Dad. She's got a funny voice. She hasn't even got a telly. She'll make us play Scrabble.'

'Look,' said Dennis, 'it's good of her to have you. So you'll do what you're told, and you'll enjoy it.'

'Oh please, Dad. Please let me stay. I'll be really good, you won't know I'm here.'

'Because you won't be here!' He was getting annoyed now. 'You're going and that's the end of it!'

Michael remembers sighing. He remembers that particular sigh. And thinking, before he opened his mouth for a third time: *This is it, I'm pushing him too far. He'll go mad this time.* But he did it anyway; he made his final quiet plea. 'But I want to stay with Mum. I want to say hello when the baby comes.'

His father didn't go mad. He softened a little. 'Come on, Michael,' he said, crouching down before him, 'it's only for two weeks. And you can say hello to the baby when you get back.'

But when he got back, the baby wasn't there.
And neither was his mum.

Michael sits in his back yard, drinking, and considers the bird box on the side of his house. The box is a shoddy oversized plywood effort, built by a previous occupant who didn't know much about birds and hadn't thought to put felt on the roof. Years of rain and sun have taken their toll and now the roof is decaying; the individual layers of the plywood are separating at the edges and have begun to spread like a fan. To Michael's knowledge, no bird has ever seen fit to go in there.

He leans forward in his deck-chair to take a closer look. *What a disaster*, he thinks, *what a mess. I'll take it down, that's what I'll do. I'll do it ... now.*

But before he can lift himself from the chair a hornet emerges through the almost round hole in the front of the box and drones off like a Lancaster bomber. Michael relaxes back into his chair and watches it fly over his unkempt garden, past his studio, and away. Two minutes later, it's back. *It's building a nest in there*, he thinks.

He looks at his watch. It's half past six. Just time for another beer before the pub opens. He goes into the house, fetches one from the fridge, and returns to the yard. Meanwhile the hornet has set out on another sortie, and when it returns again, Michael raises his drink to it.

'Cheers, hornet!' he says. 'Welcome to the neighbourhood!'

The hornet ignores him, as insects will.

Talking to insects is strange behaviour, but then Michael has had a strange day. The visit from the student has left him feeling a bit bemused. Girls usually bring out the shyness in him, but this one was different. With her easy manner, her light laugh, those trust-inducing brown eyes, she had made him feel surprisingly at ease.

She had phoned to request an interview, and her timing had been perfect, because that afternoon he'd completed an exceptionally good mount of a crow. He had no buyer for it. He had worked on it between commissions, and it was too good to sell. It was perfect, and it was for him. He was still on a high when the phone rang. He was feeling celebratory, euphoric, slightly drunk.

Even over the phone the girl sounded attractive. Her voice was confident, refined, but warm: 'Hello, Mr Marshall, I'm a Fine Art student in my final year at the University of Derby. I've been researching the representation of animals in contemporary art and I'm interested in taxidermy as a form of artistic expression. Jim Kelly at the animal sanctuary suggested I speak to you. I was wondering if it might be possible for me to come and ask you a few questions about your work?'

Michael had said, 'Yes, of course, as soon as you like.'

Which turned out to be an hour later.

By the time she arrived he was more than slightly drunk but not to the extent, he thought, that it showed. If it did, the girl seemed not to mind. She offered a slender hand, said, 'Hi, I'm Clare,' and breezed happily into his studio.

As she entered she glanced around the room, seeing a simple workspace, simply furnished, with a bare wooden floor. Pictures of animals covered the areas of whitewashed wall between the tool cabinets and shelves, together with certificates, stock sheets, lists, notes, and a poster displaying a comprehensive selection of glass eyes.

At one end of the studio a doorway led into a small showroom, at the other a huge chest freezer took up almost the entire width of the wall. Above it, in a crude glass-fronted box, was what she immediately took to be one of his earlier works – a garishly coloured stuffed pike. On top of the freezer were three empty beer cans.

As she approached Michael's bench, in the centre of the room, she shifted her attention to something else. Sitting in the middle of the bench, mounted in a plain wooden case, was the crow. A small brass plate on the front of the case carried the word 'Crow.' There was no date, and no name.

She looked at Michael, who was temporarily absorbed with the figure of the bird. She studied the side of his clean-shaven face, and when he turned towards her she saw the pride in his eyes.

'Do you like it?' he asked.

'Yes,' she said. 'It's quite something.'

He reached out and gently stroked the crow's wing with the back of his hand. 'Do you know much about birds?'

'Not really.'

'Well,' he said, 'this particular crow is a carrion crow. Do you know what carrion means?'

'Isn't it dead flesh?'

'That's right,' said Michael. 'Also something vile or filthy, according to the dictionary. As an adjective it means rotten, loathsome.'

She glanced away, the smile she had entered with still playing on her lips. 'I see.'

'But,' he continued, 'look at this bird! This is one of our most beautiful birds. It's sleek, it's uncomplicated, it's black – it's got none of the easy beauty that colour can give. No, the crow has a darker beauty, a beauty more dependent on form, attitude, texture.'

'Yes,' said Clare, 'I think you're right.' She studied the bird for a moment, then took a notebook from her bag, opened it, and looked expectantly at Michael.

'Oh,' he said. 'Oh, yes, you've got some questions. Hang on a minute, I'll go and grab a couple of chairs from the house. I won't be long.'

He left the studio and Clare waited silently for his return, thinking through her questions. She was hoping to reassure herself that her dissertation, which she had submitted some weeks ago, was essentially OK, as she was starting to suspect that it wasn't. The feeling of intellectual anxiety which had been hovering on the outer edges of her consciousness for several days was all too familiar. She knew she would never be the world's greatest artist or the world's brightest student. Ever since she had plucked up the courage to join her Foundation Art course, some five years ago, she had been aware that others in the class grasped concepts more quickly than she did, that they saw more clearly, felt more instinctively. It had continued all through university. Whilst her flatmate, Jaz, had never once considered the idea that her future held anything but life as a professional painter, Clare secretly aspired to continuing the family tradition of teaching. Her father was headmaster of a small school back in Cornwall, her elder brother had emigrated to Australia where he now taught English, and she too could see herself in the role. She would picture herself, sometimes, standing in front of the children, teaching them to grasp, to see, to feel.

When Michael returned she outlined her dissertation to him. 'The main emphasis,' she said, 'was on the use of live animals in conceptual art, but my research also showed an increasing use of taxidermy techniques by artists in recent years. I mean, it started with the stuff we've all heard about, like Damien Hirst's *Away from the flock* – you know, the sheep in the tank of formaldehyde? – but there's all kinds of other strands and ideas that have developed from there.'

'OK,' said Michael carefully, 'so where do I come in?'

Clare hesitated. 'I don't know, quite. It's just, I've essentially argued that the very *actuality* of real animals, their absolute presence, seems to overshadow the artist's creative content a lot of the time. Does that make sense?'

'Maybe,' said Michael. 'But then taxidermy – true taxidermy I mean – is a craft, not an art. Because taxidermy is about the animal, and art is about humans. Take the Hirst example. You're not looking at an animal when you view that piece – the sheep might as well be made of clay.'

'How can you say that?' she said. 'Yes, art's anthropocentric, that's inevitable. Otherwise it couldn't mean anything to us. But in Hirst's work the presence of the animal is an essential part of the constructed meaning, isn't it?'

'No.'

'Because?'

'Because it's the idea of the animal, and nothing more. Hirst practically spells it out in the titles he gives those pieces. *Away from the flock* – that's not about a sheep, any more than *Mother and child divided* is about cows.'

'But Hirst said those pieces were designed, in part, to force us to examine society's relationship with animals.'

'We don't have one. That's my point. And when we discover ourselves in them, we deny what they are. Do you see?'

'I'm not sure,' said Clare. 'I think so. Which leaves me more uncertain about it all than I was before I came.' She managed an ironic smile. 'So thanks for that.'

There was a brief awkward silence during which they both found themselves gazing once more at the crow.

'Would you mind,' said Clare, after a moment, 'if we forgot the questions for a bit? I think I'd like to do some sketching.'

'Of course!' said Michael, failing to conceal his pleasure. 'Do you want peace and quiet or am I all right to do a bit of tidying up?'

'Oh, please do.'

'Right,' he said, and he pottered happily around the studio, clearing away the empty cans, rearranging a shelf, sorting through his order book, while Clare prepared her things and proceeded to sketch the crow. The soft stroking of pencil on paper and the sounds of Michael's gentle rearrangements brought an atmosphere of total calm to the studio, a welcome reprieve from the outside world. Neither of them said anything, but they both felt it.

4

Gypsy jumps up onto Dennis's lap and licks his face. It's time for their walk, and she wants to get on with it.

He pushes her away gently. 'Soon,' he says.

She jumps back down onto the carpet, but continues to dance madly around his feet. She's three quarters Jack Russell terrier, one quarter poodle, and a full four quarters of furry white enthusiasm. She's been his companion for the last seven years, and every day of those seven years, just before teatime, they have been for that walk.

Dennis sighs heavily. It's been getting harder and harder lately to summon up the strength to leave the house. He's been feeling increasingly tired, and has been needing to use his inhaler more than ever. He has also been bringing up unusually large amounts of phlegm. Yesterday he noticed what looked like a trace of blood.

Dennis has emphysema, or 'smoker's lung'. It's not surprising – he's smoked twenty or more cigarettes a day since his late teens. He's damaged his body irrevocably, and things are only going to get worse. The alveoli, the multitude of tiny air sacs clustered at the end of his airways, deep within his lungs, are losing their natural elasticity, which once made exhaling an easy, unconsidered act. Now, more and more, he has to force the air out of himself, with the same deliberate effort that he makes to draw it in. But his airways were not designed to have the air forced back through them, as they were not designed to be filled with the smoke from his cigarettes, and they are protesting. Or, rather, they are giving up, surrendering to these unnatural pressures.

Although the capacity of Dennis's lungs is decreasing, their overall size steadily grows, as each day tens of thousands of alveoli harden and swell and join the ranks of the converted. His frame is adapting to this growth, and he has already developed the distended, barrel-like chest that typifies the disease.

Without knowing it, Dennis has taught himself a number of tricks to help him adapt to his situation. He has taught himself economy of expression, how not to waste words. If a gesture will suffice, then he doesn't speak at all. A raised flattened hand, like a policeman stopping traffic, means, 'Can't talk. Need to breathe.'

This suits Gypsy well enough. With the exception of her own name – which she's always pleased to hear – she doesn't care much for words anyway. But she does care for her daily walk, she cares very much for it, and it's time, it's definitely time. She leaps back up onto Dennis, and she nuzzles at his ear, and she slobbers down the side of his face.

This time he doesn't push her away. He wipes the slobber from his cheek with the palm of his hand. He runs his stubby fingers through the silky tufts of fur that sprout from the top of her head, and he scratches the back of her neck, and he just can't help but smile.

'Gypsy,' he says.

5

Phil is the Lead Mortgage Advisor at a bank in Derby. He's been married to Kate for almost twenty years. They live on a new estate on the outskirts of Woodington with their two children: Nathan, who's fourteen, and Emily, who's twelve. Most Saturday afternoons Michael spends over at their house. They asked him around for tea once, a few years ago, for no reason in particular, and he's been going ever since.

Phil and Michael are not the same, they were never going to be. But they are brothers, after all. They've shared some kind of a life, and they ought to be able to at least enjoy a beer or two together. They have an unspoken agreement that they won't talk of much beyond the weather, or what's on the television, or how the beer tastes. On the whole, this arrangement works quite well.

There are times, though, when Phil can't help himself, and he'll give in to his ordinary need to tell Michael all about his latest promotion at the bank, or his new car, or his plans for a loft conversion. Michael hates it when that happens. He hates the sadness that envelops them both at that moment when, halfway through a sentence about turnover or nought to sixty or the price of pine panelling, Phil realises that he's done it again, that he's telling Michael things he just can't hear.

At other times – and this is worse – Michael's the one to forget himself. Maybe he's halfway through a commission and he's had to drag himself away from his bench and he can't quite leave it behind. And he's sitting there pretending to watch the telly but he can see the animal in his head and he's thinking: *OK, this fox – this particular fox – what's he doing? What's he thinking? Is he scared?*

Should he be?

And Kate wanders in from the kitchen and asks if he'd like another drink but he doesn't notice her because he's not sure how much we should see of this fox's teeth, and he needs to be. He needs to be sure.

'Another drink? Michael, would you like another?'

And this time he hears her and the fox hears her too and it bolts off into the dark and Michael is angry and he says, 'Yes please, another drink would be nice.'

'You were miles away.'

He still is, but he's trying to pull himself back. 'Mmm, I was thinking about something I'm working on. I'm not completely sure of how to present it yet.'

'Oh, I see,' says Kate, and she goes off to get the drink.

There's an odd silence now, despite the TV, and Phil thinks he ought to say something, so he asks: 'What's the problem?'

Michael begins to explain, as he's done so many times before. About how a taxidermist doesn't just 'do' an animal. About how you have to empathise with the animal, respect it. How each individual creature is unique, each with its own personality. He tries to keep it casual and simple, tries to talk the way Phil does, but already he's beginning to shift on the sofa, beginning to pull himself upright.

He goes beyond the one fox and into his work in general. He says, 'It's all about observation. You've got to observe. You've got to capture the details that ordinary eyes can't see.'

He's leading himself into his passion now and it animates him and before he knows it he's up off the sofa. He says, 'You've got to understand form,' and his hands sweep form into the air. He says, 'You've got to understand biology,' and his hands hold the weight of invisible bones.

He says, 'You've got to understand life.'

And he's standing there, all caught up in it, and the first finger of his right hand is pointing straight at Phil's face and it's happened again. Because Michael's mouth may be saying other things but that finger is saying: *You – you with your tedious little job and your DIY and your new fucking Audi – you'll never understand anything.*

6

'Jaz, are you awake?'

'What?'

'Are you awake?'

'Erm, yes, I am now. What time is it?'

'Ten to one.'

'Oh.'

'I can't sleep.'

'Right.'

'Look, if –'

'Clare, for God's sake!'

Clare sits on the edge of Jaz's bed. Jaz props herself up against the headboard and turns on the bedside lamp, which casts a fringed oval of light over the covers. She looks into Clare's eyes with concern. 'What is it?'

'Nothing much. I don't know.'

'Man trouble?'

'No.'

'Not our Andrew again? Please say it's not Andrew.'

'It's nothing to do with Andrew.'

'Who, then?'

'Honestly, it's not that kind of thing.'

'So, if it's not a man problem, what is it?'

Clare sighs. 'Well, you know that taxidermist I went to interview the other day?'

'Yes?'

'It's to do with that, kind of. We started talking about my dissertation, and he made a couple of comments.'

'Oh?'

'And the upshot is, I've realised my dissertation is rubbish. I've been looking at it on the PC and it's rubbish. I've made some really basic mistakes and it's too late to do anything about it now. All that work I put into it, and I just know it's no good. I really wish I'd spoken to him earlier.'

'I'm sure it's not as bad as all that,' says Jaz.

'It is. It's going to affect my degree results, big time.'

'You don't know that. You're just feeling the pressure. It's natural.' She pauses. 'So, how old was he? Did he have a goatee? I always imagine them with a goatee.'

'What?'

'Your taxidermist.'

'I'm talking about my work.'

'And I want to know about the taxidermist. What was he like?'

Clare shakes her head gently, resigning herself to Jaz's curiosity. 'He was ... nice. A bit shy, perhaps, but nice.'

'How old?'

'Not very. Maybe thirty-five. He's very good at what he does, very passionate. I ended up doing a bit of sketching. I've arranged to go back in a couple of weeks and do a bit more. And he hasn't got a beard, goatee or otherwise.'

'Good,' says Jaz. 'I've never liked beards.'

'I don't mind men with beards,' says Clare. 'It's boys with beards I can't stand. Boys who think a bit of fluff on their chin somehow proves something.'

Jaz looks past her bedroom door into the greenly lit landing. 'Like my brother, you mean?'

'Yes,' says Clare, softly. 'I suppose.'

There's a moment's silence, then Jaz says, 'You know, I never did get the full story. I got bits from you and bits from Andrew, but I still don't really know what happened. One minute you seemed so happy, and then ... '

Clare sighs again. 'Oh, it was nothing big, nothing specific. It might have seemed sudden to you but really it wasn't. It had been building for weeks, months.'

'Go on.'

'I'd rather not.'

'But I want you to.'

Clare hesitates. 'Well, what started it was, we'd had this argument about what he'd call a piece of "direct action". They were sending letters to the director of a laboratory, saying they were going to hurt him if he didn't put a stop to what the company was doing.'

'Hurt him how?'

'Physically.'

'How physically?'

'I don't know. To me the details made no difference. I just thought it was wrong to be making threats like that, it was cowardly. But the thing is ... Oh, can we talk about this some other time, Jaz?'

'No, Clare, this sounds like something I should hear.'

'I don't want to.'

'And I didn't particularly want to be woken up at one o'clock in the morning, did I?'

'Then don't make too much of this, all right?'

'I won't.'

'OK. Well, the thing is, whenever Andrew spoke about something being done to that man, there was ... '

'What?'

Clare reaches out and takes Jaz's hands into her own. 'There was pleasure in his voice, Jaz. I realised he was enjoying the thought of what they might do to him.'

Jaz gently withdraws her hands and folds them on her lap. 'No,' she says, firmly, 'I don't believe that. He's never been violent.'

Clare stares dully at the foot of the bed. 'Not outwardly, maybe. But I saw it in his eyes, and I heard it in his voice. And it ... scared me.'

For a long time Jaz doesn't respond. She toys abstractedly with the emerald pendant that hangs around her neck and her eyes map the walls without seeing them. Eventually she says, 'So did you talk to him about it?'

'No,' says Clare. 'I didn't need to. I just knew I couldn't love him any more.'

'And that was that?'

'Yes.'

'So what did you tell him? How did you end it?'

'Very ineffectively. I told him about something James gave to me, at the airport, when he left for Australia. We were standing in Departures and I was crying, I couldn't help myself. I wanted to smile and wish him a good journey and tell him I'd write and pretend it was no big deal, but I couldn't pull it off, and I was crying because I was losing my big brother, because he wouldn't be there to look after me any more. Which I know is pathetic, by the way. Anyway, James said, "Don't cry, I'll only be a phone call away," and all the usual things, and then he said, "Hey, I've just remembered; read this," and he dug inside that old suede jacket of his and passed me some folded up paper. "It's a short story," he said. "It's beautiful!" And he hugged me and kissed me and swept off to his new life.'

Jaz is smiling now, drawn, despite herself, into the scene. 'So what was the story?'

'It was by someone called Ali Smith – a Scottish writer.'

'And?'

'And it *was* beautiful.'

'So what was it about?'

'It was about lots of things,' says Clare, oblivious to Jaz's impatience. 'But they were all summed up in one sentence.'

'Which was?'

'*Look upon the world with love.*'

'So how,' asks Jaz, cautiously, 'does this tie in with Andrew?'

'Well,' says Clare, 'I read the story that night, and I read it again. Then I put it down. Then I re-read it the next day.'

'Yes?'

'There's a woman in it – a French teacher who has a nervous breakdown, right there in the classroom, in front of all of the kids. And the kids start taking advantage, they start writing dirty words on the blackboard, getting braver and braver, because she doesn't say anything to stop them. She just stares out of the window, frozen.'

'And?'

'And it all goes on, and there's a couple of sensitive kids who get a feeling for what's happening, but the rest don't, and they think they can do what they like and then all of a sudden the teacher comes away from the window, rubs their stuff off the blackboard, writes something of her own, and makes them all pay attention.'

'And it's –'

'*Look upon the world with love.* Which struck me then, and now, as one of those lines that says everything.'

Jaz falls back into silence for a moment, then she says quietly, 'OK, I think I know what you're saying.'

Clare smiles bitterly. 'Andrew didn't.'

'No,' said Jaz. 'I'm sure.'

Clare yawns, suddenly sleepy, and takes her friend's hands for a second time. 'You know I'd never hold Andrew's actions against you, don't you?'

'Of course,' says Jaz.

'I know it's awkward for you. I expect you to love him, the same as I love James.'

'We've just got things the wrong way round haven't we?' says Jaz. 'Andrew here, causing us grief, and your James in Oz.'

'He should never have gone. I miss him so much.'

'I know. You were really close weren't you?'

'We still are close, we're just not near.'

'Yeah.'

'Anyway, I might have a plan to get over there myself.'

'Really?'

'It's a possibility.'

'Let's hear it, then.'

'Another time, Jaz, eh? I'm tired now.'

'All right. You get yourself to bed. And don't worry about your dissertation – I'm sure it'll be fine.'

'OK,' says Clare. 'Goodnight.'

'Goodnight, Clare.'

7

Michael's father has come to visit him. He can't remember the last time this happened. In fact, he's fairly sure it never has.

Dennis sits himself down in a corner of the studio. Gypsy is up by the house, tied to a drainpipe, whining.

'Don't want ... to disturb,' Dennis says. 'Pretend not here.'

But he is here, and Michael doesn't like it. Because having him here brings out the little boy in him, who must impress, who must get it right. It distracts him, and makes him strangely nervous.

Michael is sewing up the skin of a small bird. It's the size and shape of a fat sparrow, but there the similarity ends. Because a sparrow – even to Michael, who will look at a sparrow closely – is a plain, humble and unassuming creature. This bird is none of those things.

This bird has a brick-red face, fearlessly intense eyes, an inky black shadow of a beard. It's got a fine, smooth, russet-coloured breast, a belly the lightest of greys, a yellow-tipped tail, with a shocking scarlet underside, and purple wings with small red globules stuck to them, as if some of the feathers have been dipped into sealing wax.

'Strange bird,' says Dennis. 'What –'

'It's a waxwing,' says Michael. *It's a waxwing and how can I pretend you're not here if you're going to start asking questions?*

'From?'

'Scandinavia.'

'Scandinavia?'

'Yes, Dad.'

Dennis is silent as Michael finishes the sewing. Then he says:

'Why not ... someone in Scandinavia ... do it?'

Michael shakes his head in despair. 'Because when it was in Scandinavia it was still flying around, that's why. Then it made its way over here, managed to get itself killed, and came to me.'

Dennis raises his dark eyebrows. 'Flew?'

'Yes.'

'All way from –'

'Yes.' *For fuck's sake.*

'Oh.' Dennis lets out a deep sigh and sinks further into his chair. 'I see.'

Michael takes the bird into the showroom and puts it to one side. It's the first waxwing he's ever done and it's essential that he gets it right. He's never seen one in the wild, most of his knowledge of them has come from books. He knows that they feed on fruit – a shortage of which further east is bringing them to Britain – and that flocks of them have been known to strip a holly bush bare in seconds. His books tell him this, and there are photographs too, but Michael needs to know more than these words and pictures can convey. He needs to know how this handsome marauder would describe itself, if it could talk as well as it once sang. When he knows that, he'll be ready to present the bird.

If Dennis wasn't there he would ask the bird straight. It's what he's always done with animals he doesn't properly know. He would cradle the creature in his hands, look into its eyes and say the words out loud: 'Who are you?'

Michael lingers in the showroom for a while, as he thinks about this. He's aware of the irony. He can talk to a dead bird, but he can't talk to his own father.

Back in the studio he looks for something to do that won't require too much concentration. He's feeling less and less happy about having his father there – watching and breathing – but he doesn't want to stop work altogether. He's got a backlog of commissions several weeks long and more work coming in all the time.

There's a completed tawny owl that's ready for casing up. The owl is to be presented perched on an oak branch, with a single leaf attached. The branch and the leaf have been freeze-dried, and the leaf recoloured with acrylic paints. The bird, branch and leaf have been fastened together. All Michael has to do now is fix them into the case.

Normally, it would be a simple task. But his disquiet is escalating and with a shock he sees his hand begin to tremble as he tries to insert the assembly. *Jesus Christ, he's only my father, why should I tremble?* But he can't make the hand still, can't stop it shaking. And he can't stop working because he has to impress. And he catches the leaf on the side of the case and it breaks away from its stem.

In a moment, the leaf's carefully manufactured appearance of suppleness and life is betrayed by its dry reality, by its real self. It flutters and twists – devoid now of any grace – down towards the floor, a piece of dead material.

Michael watches it fall. He can hear the sound of his father's laboured breathing, and a banging beneath his own ribs. Then his own voice, screaming, 'That's it! That's fucking it! You've done it now! You've really done it now!'

In all his life Michael has never sworn in front of his father. But the swearing is the least of it. He stands frozen by the bench.

At first Dennis does nothing, says nothing. Then, groaning beneath his breath, he lifts himself from his chair, walks slowly over, bends down, and picks up the leaf.

'Where's the glue?' he says.

Michael doesn't answer.

Again: 'Where's the glue?'

Michael composes himself, says in a small, hoarse voice, 'It's not as simple as that.'

'But –'

'Look,' says Michael, 'it's all right. Leave it. You'll not be able to do it.'

He takes the leaf from his father, places it to one side, and says, 'How about a cup of tea?'

Dennis nods.

Michael goes to fill the kettle.

Later, as they sit silently drinking, Michael eyes his father over the rim of his mug. He knows he should have let him stick the leaf back on, that his refusal had been an act of insensitivity. But then, he deserved it. Because what is he, if not insensitive, this man who has always shown more affection to his dogs than to his sons, who has always denied them the memory of their mother by refusing even to even her name uttered?

8

When Nancy died everyone said that Dennis would have to give up the farm. Eileen came down from Edinburgh, and she said it too. 'It'll be too much for you, Dennis, trying to keep the business alive and looking after two young boys at the same time. You ought to buy a house up in Woodington, and get yourself a nice steady nine-to-five job. In fact, you could have a word up at the Water Board, and ask them to bear you in mind. I hear the wages are quite good.'

'Oh, no,' Dennis had said. 'There's no way I'm giving up the farm. And if I did you wouldn't catch me working up there. It was them that took away my last farm, in case you've forgotten.'

Dennis had never forgiven the Water Board for what they had done to his and Eileen's childhood home. He had taken it for granted that the rest of his life would revolve around Furnace Farm, nestled in the bottom of Calke Valley, with the fields sloping up gently on either side of the house, the trout flashing and rolling in the brook that ran beside it, and the falcons gliding through the vast skies above.

He never forgot the time he first heard of a scheme for turning the biggest part of the valley into a reservoir. He was eighteen years old, and enjoying a pint of bitter in the Woodington Arms, when Jed Robey, a dairy farmer from a nearby village, added his voice to the rumour. Dennis had laughed it off as nothing more than ridiculous gossip. For generations his ancestors had scratched their will into the surface of those valley fields. They had ploughed and harrowed and rolled the earth, they had turned it into some of the most productive land in the area. No one had the right to throw them off. It couldn't happen.

Jed thought otherwise. 'The region's getting short of water,' he said. 'That is a simple fact. And you, young Dennis, of all people, should know the value of water. Is it not water, after all, that makes things grow?'

Dennis knew he was being baited, but he said nothing.

'And water can't be stored just anywhere, can it?' Jed continued. 'It needs holding on all sides, it needs a vessel.' He brought his calloused hands together, formed them into the shape of a rowing boat, and held them out in front of him. 'Look at the shape of Calke Valley,' he said. 'Look in particular at how it tapers away and rises towards Five Lanes End. It would only take a good strong dam on this side and there is your vessel, there is your reservoir. Carr's Brook would handle the overflow quite nicely ... '

'Dennis?' said Eileen.

'What?'

'We were talking about what you're going to do.'

'No, Eileen, you were talking about it. And I've told you, I'm not leaving the farm. Market gardening is what I do. It's what our family has been doing for the last six generations. Or have you forgotten that as well?'

Eileen shook her head sadly. 'Dennis, I swear, I haven't forgotten anything. But it's a changing world, and you've got to change with it.'

'But gardening's all I know, Eileen, and it's all I want. And when the boys are older, it'll be there for them, too.'

'Oh, Dennis,' she sighed. 'Oh, Dennis, it won't. Can't you see what's happening around you? The world is getting smaller. When I go into my local supermarket I can buy tomatoes from Holland, and lettuce from Spain, and I do. I do buy them, and so does everyone else. And ten years from now there'll be a supermarket in every town, getting their tomatoes from Holland and their lettuce from Spain.

30

And their potatoes, and their sprouts, and their carrots. There'll even be a supermarket in Woodington one day.'

'Don't be ridiculous!'

'It'll happen. It'll be the supermarkets calling all the shots soon. And the people who run the supermarkets are only concerned with one thing, Dennis – profit. They'll be buying their stuff from abroad, even cheaper than the English can grow it, and they'll not lose any sleep over the plight of a widower with two young sons to raise.'

'No,' said Dennis. 'No, we'll be all right. People will always want good home-grown stuff. They always have and they always will.'

'Dennis, you've got blinkers the size of dustbin lids. Why do you think it was so easy for them to flood the valley in the first place? The land just isn't needed like it was. How many market gardeners did this area have a hundred years ago? Seventy? Eighty? And how many are there now? Five! And I heard this morning that Millers out on The Common are in trouble. They ploughed eight acres of cabbage under only last week. Eight acres! How long can they carry on like that?'

Dennis had no answer. He only knew that he wasn't going to leave the farm. He pulled a half-smoked cigarette from behind his ear, put it in his mouth, and lit it. He took a heavy drag, held it within him as long as he could, then released it, forcing the smoke between his barely open lips, blowing it across the room in a slow, steady stream.

Eileen spoke quietly now. 'I don't mean to lecture you, Dennis,' she said. 'I just think you should consider all the options, now that things have changed. I want you to think about it, that's all. Life isn't just about work.'

She didn't say any more. The other things she wanted to say would have to wait. It was too late now, she'd upset him, at a time when she should have been comforting him.

Perhaps, later, he would think about it.

But she guessed, correctly, that he wouldn't.

9

The hornet strips the soft wood from the fence posts at the edge of Michael's tangled garden. She leaves tiny elongated marks on the timber; temporary, benign scars, such as a lover's fingernails leave on willing flesh. She chews the wood, makes of it a gluey pulp, and returns with it to her new home.

She has something of the Ancient Greeks about her, in her primal mask of a face, in her talent for construction. With an infinite lightness of touch she applies and spreads the wood paste, invoking, and creating, the geometry of nature. She has almost completed the initial chamber, a perfect sphere containing six hexagonal cells that will cradle the first batch of eggs.

Eggs which within days of being laid will burst at the seams, releasing their wriggling contents. Larvae, which will need to be fed. Food, more food. We're hungry, bring us more.

The hornet will fly to and fro until her wings ache, searching for scraps of meat, for lesser insects, for nourishment for her babies. If insects could think, she would think a woman's work is never done.

But she would be wrong. Because although she has no way of knowing, those demanding larvae will soon become smaller versions of herself, an army of daughters that will take over the job of expanding the nest. They will rear the young, they will tend the sick, and she will spend the rest of her days in relative ease. External sources of danger – birds, humans, English weather – will be of no concern to her. She will remain in the nest, a servant only of her genes.

What must it be like to be her? A wholly natural creature, wholly a part of nature? Nature, which is unknowing, yet all-knowing? Nature, which doesn't think, but does?

What must it be like to just do, with no thoughts of why you are doing, with no thoughts of whether or not you should? To have a purpose, and for that purpose to be enough?

Sometimes, when Michael is lost in his work, he seems to find the answer. Maybe he's applying the final touches to a specimen, preening the feathers of a bird, perhaps. He's got a fine pair of tweezers, laying back the feathers like tiles on a roof, teasing and coaxing them into position, attaining perfection in every fibre, bringing life to the lifeless. At times like this – which can last for hours – he forgets himself; he disappears; he's gone.

But it can't last forever, this absence, this non-feeling. Sooner or later it slips away. Because no one can work all the time. They have to live, too.

So now he's sitting in his kitchen, trying to live. And he's bored and depressed, he doesn't know what to do with himself. And there's something else. The student girl, Clare. It's five days since her visit and he can't stop thinking about her. Every time the phone rings, he hopes it's her. Some vital question she forgot to ask, something that can't wait till next week? Every knock on the door, he hopes it's her. *I didn't leave my fountain pen here, by any chance? I seem to have lost it and I happened to be passing and ...*

All of which is ridiculous. Because women and him, it never quite works out. And he knows why. It's because he isn't good at sharing things, isn't good at sharing himself. And, yes, he's obsessive about his work. The last girlfriend he had – almost six years ago now – accused him of thinking more of his animals than he did of her. It was an ordinary, clichéd thing to say, and like most clichés it hit the nail squarely on the head. So he admitted it. He told her: 'Yes you're right, I do, I think more of my animals than anything.' She finished with him on the spot.

But, still, this Clare ...

He sighs, wanders across to the radio, turns it on. Willy Nelson is singing about how his woman left him because he didn't treat her right. He turns it back off. He goes over to the fridge. It's a bit early in the day but perhaps just the one?

As he's closing the fridge door, can in hand, he glances at the floor. The floor's covered with lino tiles, each tile half light, half dark. It occurs to him, not for the first time, that there are two ways of seeing the pattern – as areas of darkness surrounded by light, or areas of light surrounded by the dark. He sees the latter and shakes his head, irritated with himself for reading deep things into lino. *Floor tiles, for fuck's sake. What's the matter with me? Why can't I live?*

Clare is sketching the crow again, this time from a different perspective. Her eyes are on the bird, but she's aware of occasional glances from the other side of the studio, where Michael is tidying his tool cupboard. There's the same feeling of calm in the room that she felt during her last visit and she breathes it in, gratefully.

'So,' Michael says eventually, 'how are your studies coming along?'

'They're almost finished,' she says. 'In a couple of weeks it'll all be over.'

'It must be a busy time, then.'

'It is. I'm too busy to be here, strictly speaking.' She looks across at him, there's a pause, then she says, 'I'm a bit concerned, actually. I've come this far and suddenly I seem to have lost my focus. Or rather, I'm beginning to see I never really had one. It's like, with my dissertation, the more I think about it the less persuasive I think it was.'

Michael moves away from the cupboard and leans his back against the wall, his arms loosely folded. 'So, tell me again – you were looking at the use of animals in modern art?'

'Conceptual art.'

'OK. From what angle?'

'Well, I started with the general thought of, you know, looking at why artists had chosen to use animals in various installations. Then I found that there's this huge argument going on about whether or not animals should be being used at all. You know, the morality of it. Whether it's exploitative, whether the ends justify the means and so on. So I thought I'd concentrate on that. And it was interesting, in that I found lots of material to discuss, lots of ways of looking at things, but that's almost the problem somehow. I'm beginning to think that some of the artists were so concerned with their work being open to interpretation that they absolved themselves of responsibility, including responsibility to the animals. It's almost as if they were sidestepping the central issue. Does that make sense?'

'I think so, yes.'

'For example, there was an artist a few years ago who caused all kinds of controversy with a piece that involved ten kitchen blenders, half filled with water, each with a live goldfish swimming in it. Did you hear about it?'

'No.'

'Well, the blenders were all connected to the mains, and there was a notice telling members of the public that if they wanted to turn them on, they could do.'

'And someone did?'

'Yes. Two of them. Two goldfish killed, in the name of art.'

'And?'

'And it caused a lot of anger. It got seized by the police, he got taken to court.'

'Right.'

'But then someone else, an influential animal rights philosopher, stood up and said it was an important piece, raising profound questions about our power over animals!'

'Well –'

'But if you follow that argument to its logical conclusion you could encourage someone to kill a child, and say you were raising profound questions about our power over children!'

Michael frowns. 'Yes, I suppose if you look at it that way ... So what did the artist himself have to say about it?'

'That he was trying to test visitors' sense of right and wrong.'

'Oh.'

'So, anyway, you had the debate, you had the art doing what it should, making people ask questions, and in the centre of it you had the goldfish, but no one was actually looking at them any more. And I realise now that what you said about Hirst's work applies to that piece, and to practically every other piece I'd written about. The animal has been replaced by the idea.'

She indicates the subject of her sketching. 'And then I look at this crow, the actuality of it, the presence of it, and I can't see anything else, and I don't want to. Because it's not about me. It's aloof and, I don't know, better, somehow. Does that sound crazy?'

Michael smiles and says, 'Only the bit about it being better than you.' Then he turns quickly back to his tool cupboard so she can't see his face.

Clare sits silently for a few moments, touched by Michael's boyish compliment. Then she stands up, and steps away from the bench. Her attention shifts briefly to the sky beyond the window, then – as a thought occurs – to Michael.

'Who buys all your work?' she says. 'I was under the impression that taxidermy was a bit of a dying trade. I mean, I'd always associated stuffed animals with stately homes and old-fashioned pubs. There can't be that much demand nowadays, surely?'

'Well,' says Michael, 'it depends how you look at it. There probably isn't the demand that there used to be, but if you have a good enough reputation you'll get the commissions. It's not just the stately homes that are interested, either, although I've done a fair bit of work for the National Trust over the years. There are lots of private collectors out there too, more than you'd imagine. And there are theatres and TV companies. I supplied a brace of pheasants for a stage production of *Lady Chatterley's Lover* a few weeks ago, and the BBC bought a fox.'

'A fox?'

'Yes, for a new drama series they're making. I had to make it look as if it had been caught in a gin trap. The idea is that some kids get to find it while they're out playing in the fields.'

'That's terrible,' says Clare. 'Some poor fox being sacrificed for yet another lame countryside drama.'

There's something in her voice that Michael finds wounding, but he pushes the feeling aside and tells her, gently, that it's not like that. 'Taxidermy,' he says, 'is about preservation, not destruction, and we're only allowed to preserve animals that have already died through other causes. It's the golden rule, the regulations are very strict. In the USA – where taxidermy is absolutely huge, by the way – the laws are even tighter. You're not even allowed to pick up a dead bird from the side of the road. It's perfectly legal to go up into the hills and shoot a cougar, mind you, but that's America for you.'

'Oh,' says Clare. 'So, where do you get your animals from?'

'Well, people are bringing them to me all the time. That fox, for example, had been hit by a car. Then there are birds of prey that have flown into power lines, or have died from secondary poisoning – that's when they've eaten rats that have been poisoned by farmers or whatever. Jim at the sanctuary passes on the animals they're unable to save. I get my specimens from all over the place, and any I can't do immediately just go into the freezer until I can get round to them.'

'So,' says Clare, 'you're telling me that you've never deliberately killed an animal, or had one killed, just so you could preserve it?'

A strange expression appears on Michael's face, and he glances briefly up towards the odd-looking stuffed pike on the wall above his deep freeze. She looks too, and notices for the first time a small blue button where the fish's eye should be.

'Only once,' he says, 'when I was young.'

Michael is very drunk. It's eleven o'clock at night, and he's standing in his studio, in front of the freezer, gazing up at the stuffed pike. His body is swaying, and his eyes won't focus. He tries to fix his eyes on the pike, tries to make it still, whilst all around him the room swims.

'I've met a girl,' he says. 'I can't stop thinking about her.'

He waits for a few moments, as if allowing time for a response.

'She's a student. Fine Art. She's been here twice, her name's Clare. I can't stop thinking about her. I've already said that, haven't I?'

He's got a half bottle of whisky, his second of the evening. He lifts it up to his mouth, takes a swig, and wipes his lips with the back of his hand. 'I've already said it, yes, I know. Yes.'

His legs waver beneath him, and he slips backwards. The small of his back bangs against the edge of his workbench, but he doesn't feel it. The bottle drops from his hand, and he bends down and scrabbles to retrieve it. By the time he has, half of the contents have glugged away, and are soaking into the floor boards.

'Fuck,' he says, straightening up.

He lifts his face back up to the pike. 'Sorry, Mum. Mustn't swear. Mustn't swear like that. You never did like that kind of language, did you? I remember.' He drops his head. 'I remember.'

He hoists himself up onto the bench. 'That's better,' he says. 'Takes the weight off.'

The bench is strewn with countless tiny particles of polyurethane foam, shavings from a block that he was using earlier in the day to form the inner body of a rabbit. He rubs his fingers across the surface of the bench, feeling the particles roll and crush beneath them. He lifts the bottle and takes another swig.

'You know, Mum,' he says, 'I've often wondered if it would happen again, if I would meet someone who'd make me feel ... who'd make me feel that it was worth the effort, worth going through it all. You won't believe this, but it's almost six years since I last had a girlfriend. You remember Janice? You remember I told you about her? You'd have liked her, I think. You'd have been pleased. But I managed to mess it up didn't I? I managed to scare her off ... '

He pauses, then he says, 'The thing is, I didn't love her. Not really, not deep down. I didn't think I could. And that's the problem, I've never loved anyone except you, Mum, and I still don't know if I can ... '

He allows a huge yawn to escape his mouth before raising the whisky bottle once more.

'But this Clare ... She's quite a bit younger than me. Ten, fifteen years maybe. I think she likes me. She's beautiful, too. She's got long dark hair. And she's got this ... openness about her, she's so easy to talk to. The first day she came, even though it was sort of an interview, I didn't feel like I was under inspection. I felt I could be myself with her. Mind you, I was a bit pissed. I mean a bit drunk. Sorry.

'She might already have a boyfriend, I don't know. But I want to know. I want to phone her up, I want to ask her out. I can't even remember how you do it ... '

His voice is beginning to slow. The whisky's hitting home.

'I even washed my van this afternoon, in case she says yes and I have to go and pick her up in it.'

He solemnly drains the last few drops from the bottle, then allows himself to recline slowly backwards on the bench until he's spread-eagled along its length.

'Not that I suppose she'd be interested in someone like me, eh, Mum? No, not someone like me.'

40

And he yawns again, and his eyes close, and he falls asleep, there on the bench.

12

The pike above Michael's freezer was the first creature that he ever preserved. It was taken from the Staunton Harold Reservoir.

At nine years old, the reservoir filled Michael with a kind of awe. The dam wall was huge and intimidating, casting a permanent shadow over the two farms, the coal yard, and the seven cottages that made up Wenleigh. A metal railing ran along the top of the wall. From the farmhouse it looked like a tightly stretched chain, holding the sides of the valley together, stopping the wound from deepening. For Michael, trying to imagine the world before the reservoir was like trying to imagine a world without a sky. The fact that his father used to live somewhere beneath it was incomprehensible.

Fishing was not permitted at the reservoir, but it went on nevertheless. Michael had often heard Phil's friends bragging of their illicit catches, their arms flung open in exaggerated approximation. Around the overflow was the place for pike, all were agreed. If you went at night and shone a lamp down into the water, you could see them basking there, the size of sharks. If Michael wanted to get himself a prize specimen, there could be no better plan than to take a midnight trip to the overflow.

Michael, though, had neither the equipment nor the ability to catch one of those big pike, whereas Phil had both. Reluctantly, Michael asked his brother's help, and to his surprise and relief, he agreed.

'Just as long as you do exactly what I tell you,' he said.

'Yes,' said Michael. 'Thank you,' said Michael.

The boys stole out of the house into a freezing February night. The cold bit at their fingers and ears as they climbed the road towards Woodington, and their breath hung about them like a warning.

Near the top of the valley Calke Road came off to the left. They crept along it as quietly as they could, keeping their mouths shut and their footsteps light. The loudest sound Michael could hear was the zip pull on his jacket beating out a tiny metal rhythm on its zip, bouncing in time to his step. Soon they would have to pass in front of the Water Board houses, where the Water Board men lived.

As they approached the first of the houses a light came on in a downstairs window, and the boys froze. Somewhere else, nearer to town, a dog began to bark. Michael's heart pounded in his chest. The sound of his breathing seemed a riot of noise.

After a few moments, the light went off.

The dog fell quiet.

And they crept on.

The road continued to rise, following its old course until it reached the end of the dam wall, where it veered off violently to the right, going on to snake its way around the edge of the water. At the end of the dam wall was a high wrought-iron gate. Behind the gate the Water Board's private service road ran along the top of the dam, eventually disappearing on the other side amidst the stark collection of concrete buildings that housed the reservoir's water treatment plant.

Michael held the fishing rod and torch while Phil climbed the gate, then he passed them through before climbing it himself. They quickly ran to the side of the road, straddled a low barrier, and dropped onto the slope of the inner wall, which was lined with large, smooth, grey stones.

A few feet below them, the water lapped restlessly against the wall. The water was huge, formidable, a world in itself. It seemed to exist in an eerie silver light of its own, enough light to make its presence known, to let them know that it was there, waiting. The boys began to pick their way along the top edge of the wall, the stones greasy and treacherous beneath their feet.

The overflow was exactly halfway along the wall, and it was several minutes before they reached it. By the time they had, they could hear the muffled sound of machinery coming from the treatment plant. A low, constant droning underpinned a more distinct humming noise which rose and fell, and rose and fell, like the breathing of a sleeping giant.

The overflow was, in effect, an enormous concrete funnel, its rim set several feet lower than the top of the dam wall. It was linked to the dam by a narrow cast iron walkway, which also ran in a circle around the rim. From this circle it was possible to see into the overflow, to see it falling and converging like a solidified whirlpool.

'It's amazing,' said Michael.

'It's an overflow,' said Phil. 'Shine that torch this way.'

Michael held the torch while Phil prepared the rod. Minutes later, Phil made the first cast, and soon after that he landed the pike.

Catching the pike was easy; killing it was the tricky bit. Michael hadn't given any thought to this aspect of things until all of a sudden there it was, thrashing around on the walkway in front of them, snapping its mouth open and shut, with Phil's hook through the side of its cheek. It was a reasonable specimen, a good twenty inches in length. Michael was half afraid that it would jerk its way through the railings and back into the water, and half afraid that it wouldn't, but Phil quickly placed the weight of his foot against the fish and trapped it lengthways against the bars.

'What do we do now?' asked Michael.

'Nothing,' said Phil.

Michael was distraught. 'But we can't just let it suffocate! We've got to put it out of its misery!'

Phil looked at him as if he were mad. 'If you want to put it out of its misery,' he said, 'there are two things you can do. Put it back in the water, or grab yourself a nice big stone off the wall and smash its skull in. But unless you want a fish with a squashed head I suggest you leave it alone. It'll die soon enough.'

Michael knew that Phil was right, but he felt suddenly sick all the same. The pike was convulsing under Phil's foot, its tail slapping violently on the deck, its head shaking a livid denial.

While the fish suffered, Michael turned away, and looked out across the reservoir. He could just about make out the silhouette of the old people's home on the far side. The lower details of the building were blurred into the landscape, but the gabled roof and slender chimneys made distinct shapes against the sky. His Aunt Eileen had once told him that she used to work there. He'd always thought of it as being miles away. Seeing it from here, he realised how close it was.

Behind him, the pike's efforts to hang on to its life were slowing. Its earlier fury had translated into a grim determination which it signalled with massive bodily jolts that decreased in frequency, but lost none of their power, right up to its last breath of unbreathable air.

And then it was dead.

13

The following afternoon, the pike lay on the draining board in the farmhouse kitchen. Michael's mother stood with her aching back against the fridge, and surveyed the shabby scene. The kitchen's worktops were old and stained. The cupboard door to her right was warped and no longer closed properly. The shelf to her left supported a shambolic collection of chipped mugs. Nancy was eight months pregnant, and feeling low.

She asked herself: *How on earth did I end up here?* Fourteen years ago, when she had become Dennis's wife, she'd looked forward to a life of steady improvement – the life he had promised her. 'Market gardening's a growing trade,' he'd said, with a smile at his own joke, and she had believed him. She had seen the farmhouse the way it could be, with sturdy handmade furniture, quarry tile floors, a welcoming fire in an open hearth.

She could barely have imagined this.

And then Michael suddenly burst in through the door, more excited than she'd ever known him, and immediately the room brightened and was just a kitchen, nothing more and nothing less. Nancy admonished herself for her selfishness, and offered her God a silent prayer of thanks.

Nancy was delighted to see Michael looking so animated for once because, despite being the youngest, he had always been the more serious of her boys. Too serious, in fact, too given to thought. And he didn't have many friends. It wasn't that he was disliked – she was sure of that – it was as if he just didn't want them, didn't need them. He preferred to be by himself, walking the surrounding fields in the hope of glimpsing the local fox, or crouching in the undergrowth at the side of the brook, watching the silver shapes flit to and fro. He was a junior member, through his school, of the Royal Society for the Protection of Birds, and could happily spend an entire afternoon in the woods, listening to their songs, contemplating their lives.

All of these things he loved to do, by himself, whilst Phil and his friends tore around the farm playing Cowboys and Indians, built dens in the haystacks, and held regular meetings of the 'Tomahawk Club,' an organisation whose chief activities, as far as Nancy could tell, were playing Cowboys and Indians and building dens in the haystacks.

Phil, Nancy knew, was doing all the things that a young boy should, and they seemed to make him happy. She imagined that it would always be this way for Phil; he'd do what he should, and it would be enough. But Michael was different. Nancy hated to use the term – he was only nine years old – but there was no other word for it: Michael was a loner.

Still, if he was a loner, he was a loner who loved his mother. He showed no signs as yet of being too old for a bedtime story, or the kiss that always followed. That much they could share. And the pike that lay on the draining board, that grotesque creature that he was so excited about, that too was something they could share, even if stuffing a fish wasn't quite Nancy's idea of a Saturday afternoon well spent.

For several nights previously, instead of Nancy reading Michael a story, they had looked together through *Practical Taxidermy,* by C.R. Hoben. It was, as its name suggested, a practical and accessible book, if not a particularly popular one – the library stamp showed that it hadn't been out on loan for almost seven years. It was an old book; most of the gold leaf on the front cover had flaked away and the author's name appeared only as the faintest of impressions in the dulled black surface. It was badly worn along the spine, which peeled away towards the top; tiny strands of black cotton straggled out from the stray edges like spiders' legs. Beneath the spine could be seen the webbing of cotton and glue that once bound it all together. It smelled of mystery and skin. It reminded Michael of the hymn books at church.

Taxidermy, it turned out, was in many ways a more simple business than Nancy had feared. And fish, luckily, were amongst the easiest of creatures to preserve. If she understood Mr Hoben correctly then, even without the various chemicals mentioned in the book, it ought to be possible to carry out a reasonably successful mount of the pike.

There were five basic steps: take the skin from the body; seal the inside of the skin with glue; stuff the skin; allow to dry; paint.

The details of the process had surprised both Michael and herself. They hadn't expected so little of an animal's internal structure to remain in a mounted specimen. Not just the flesh went, but the muscles, most of the skeleton, practically everything. All that typically remained of a creature was its skull, its teeth and its skin. Its image, and – if it was done well – its essence. And they hadn't expected the pike to need painting. But they learned, together, from the book, that the moment a fish dies its colours begin to fade.

Nancy laid out their tools on the worktop: knives, tweezers, heavy scissors. Michael fetched a long shallow box full of sand, and a bucket.

'So,' said Nancy, holding the open book towards the window to catch the light, 'first things first. Accurate colour notes, to enable lifelike reproduction of the specimen's markings.'

Michael peered at the pike, then, on a scrap of paper pulled from his pocket, he wrote: *Dark green at the top. Light green at the bottom. White bits all over.*

'Very good,' said Nancy. 'Now, what's next? Oh yes, wash the fish in a solution of salt and water to remove the mucus from its skin.'

She filled the sink with water, stirring in the salt with a large wooden spoon, and slid the fish in as far as it would go. 'We'll do the front half first,' she said, passing Michael a pair of rubber gloves, 'and then we'll turn it round.'

Michael stood beside her at the sink and together they cleaned the fish. It quickly lost its sliminess and they could soon feel the gentle rasping of its scales against their gloved fingertips. Then the water was drained away, and the fish removed.

'Good,' said Nancy. 'Now we decide which is to be the "show" side, the side which will be displayed.'

'This one,' said Michael, indicating the left side of its body.

'OK,' said Nancy. She again consulted the book and, paraphrasing it, said: 'Now a mould has to be made of the fish, so that there is a physical record of the shape of its body. This mould will be used later, to ensure that the shape of the fish is accurately reproduced when it receives its new insides. But before we make the mould we must first remove the fish's entrails and replace them with sand, to firm up and round out the body. To do this we make one curved incision, from the rear of its head, coming down along the side of the stomach, then back up the tail.'

She selected a small, sharp knife and made the incision. A quantity of deep red blood oozed out at the edges of the cut. Then, wearing the look of a woman who had gutted many fish in her lifetime but had never quite got used to the process, she opened the pike up, slid her fingers into its body and withdrew its innards. She cut away the thick strands of attached sinew with the scissors, and she and Michael grimaced in unison as the metallic smell of fish guts filled the room.

Quickly, the guts were wrapped in newspaper, and Michael was sent out with them to the dustbin. When he returned Nancy was already spooning sand into the carcass.

'Finish this off,' she said. 'I'll go and get my sewing kit.'

Michael fed more sand into the fish, eagerly and with satisfaction, as a mother feeds a small child. Then he tried to close the edges of skin back together. But he had overfilled it, overcompensated, and the two flaps refused to meet up in the middle. He pressed down on the body with the underside of his fingers, trying to force the two halves to join, but when he lifted his fingers the split remained, long and thin like a cruel smile. Hurriedly he scraped sand back out of the fish's body, wanting it to be ready for when his mother came back.

It was. 'You've made a good job of that,' she said, and she sewed the edges together.

They placed a sheet of newspaper on top of the tray of sand, and the pike was posed on the sheet, show side up. They spread its fins and fastened them into position with pins. The pike watched them with its one visible eye, a cold black bead in a ring of rusted gold.

The mould itself should have been made, according to Mr Hoben, of something known as 'No. 1 Plaster', but Michael's mould was made from a bucketful of the same material that his father used to fill in the cracks and holes that were forever appearing in the farmhouse walls.

'It's a plaster of sorts,' said Nancy, doubtfully, as she mixed powder and water into a creamy pink paste. Michael nodded, worried. If this went wrong, if the fish wouldn't come away cleanly from the mould, the whole thing would be ruined.

Together they poured the plaster over the length of the pike.

Half an hour later, the plaster was set. It had smoothed itself out over the fish like a heavy drifting of pink snow. The pins that positioned the fins pushed out into the miniature landscape like tiny telegraph poles.

Michael and his mother twisted the pins loose, and withdrew them. Then the mould, with the fish still in it, was turned over, so that the imperfect side of the fish was exposed. Nancy worked the slender fingers of her left hand beneath the exposed tip of the fish's tail, and held the mould down with her right hand, somehow managing to cross the first two fingers of it at the same time.

Michael stood pressed to her side, forgetting to breathe.

Gently, slowly, Nancy began to pull, but the pike resisted, defiant even in death. The tail fin lifted but the body proper was stuck down fast. She slid her hand under as far as she could and her fingers impressed themselves into the skin, displacing the scant flesh, until she could clearly feel the shape of the bones beneath. She was sure that it was not going to come free, that she would tear this creature in two. But she continued to lift and pull, with increasing force, until suddenly the tension released, and the pike came away in one clean movement. Its final fight was fought and lost, and Nancy yelped with pleasure as she held its body aloft.

'Yes!' said Michael, beginning to breathe again.

'Yes indeed!' said Nancy.

Now it was time for the skinning. After another brief consultation with Mr Hoben, Nancy re-moistened the fish with water, lay it on its show side, and reopened the incision, carefully cutting through the earlier stitching. First the sand was removed, and the cavity cleaned. Then it was a matter of gently working the skin away from the flesh on either side of the cut.

The skinning process was more simple than she had expected. When most of the skin had been peeled from the fish's side it was easy enough to work her fingers around, and then over, the top of the spine, and down on to the show side. By this time the inner body of the pike was already becoming a separate entity, attached to, but no longer belonging to, the skin. With the scissors she cut the bones at the bases of the fins and tail, and severed the head. The body fell away, and the skin remained.

By now, Michael was beginning to get frustrated. 'Mum,' he said, 'you're not letting me do anything!' His protest was well timed, because the sharp knife that Nancy had been using was now exchanged for the bluntest she could find.

'Clean the skin of all remaining pieces of flesh,' she said, book in hand, 'always scraping from the tail toward the head. Be careful not to injure the silvery lining next to the skin.'

Michael gingerly scraped at the skin with the knife, pausing every now and then to remove the scraps of grey-white flesh that curled up onto the side of its dull blade. It was time-consuming, but he did it well, with care. When it was finished he turned to his mother for further instruction.

'Clean the head thoroughly, and remove the eyes.'

He raised his face to her with an expression of mild horror.

'Oh, no,' she laughed. 'It's no use looking at me. That's your job.'

Michael swallowed hard. How were you supposed to take its eyes out? The book didn't say.

'I suppose you just poke them out,' said Nancy.

Michael looked at the fish, then his mother, then back at the fish. Then he slid the blunt knife in at the edge of the first eye, on the off-show side of the fish, and, grimacing, he tried to gouge it out. It wouldn't come, a transparent membrane held it in its socket. He cut through the membrane and again levered beneath the eye until suddenly it popped out, remaining attached to the fish's face by a single sinewy thread. At first, he couldn't bring himself to give it the tug needed to release it completely. Even though it had been dead since last night, and all that otherwise remained of it was its skin, Michael felt that removing the eyes was somehow a definitive act, as if up until this point he might at any moment have decided to put the pieces back together, breathe the life back in, and set the pike free.

'What's the matter, Michael?' asked Nancy.

'Nothing,' said Michael, and he snatched off the eye, and turned the fish over.

When he had removed the other eye Nancy continued: 'Now remove the cheek muscles. These can be taken out through the eye cavities. Do not remove the gills but cut away all flesh from around them, again scraping with a blunt knife if necessary. Then give the whole thing one last wash over and allow it to drain off. And while you're doing that, I'm having a sit-down.'

Michael set to work again while Nancy made her way into the sitting room. Dozens of the pike's shed scales flashed on her apron like tiny silver sequins. She lowered herself heavily into her armchair and gazed at the dead television screen in front of her, her reflection in it.

She puffed out her cheeks.

The face on the television puffed out its cheeks.

She smiled.

The face on the television smiled.

She looked up at the whitewashed wall above, at the silver-framed photograph of two people standing outside a church. Herself and Dennis, on their wedding day.

After a short while, Michael came into the room. He sat on the edge of her chair, and dropped his arm over the back, bouncing his hand against the taut fabric. 'Are you all right, Mum?'

'Yes, Michael, I'm fine.'

'We could finish it another day.'

'No, we'll finish it today, love. At least, we'll get it filled and sewn up. You won't be able to paint it until it's dried out properly. That might take a few days.'

'OK. Thanks, Mum.'

Nancy reached behind the chair to find Michael's arm and she lifted it over and held his hand in hers, resting it against the side of her swollen stomach. 'You know, don't you, Michael, that I love you very much?'

'Yes, Mum.'

'And that the new baby won't change anything?'

'Yes.'

'And that I'll always be here for you, whenever you need me?'

'Yes.'

She squeezed his hand. 'That's good.'

He leaned towards her, and rested his head against hers.

'I've been thinking,' he said. 'What are we going to do for the fish's eye? It says to use a glass one in the book, but where will we get one from?'

'That, my son, is a very good question. But don't worry about it, we'll find one from somewhere. And in the meantime, so we're not having to look at an empty eye socket, which I have to say I find a bit eerie, we'll use ... ' She dipped her right hand into her apron pocket and removed a small blue button. 'This button, which fell off my coat this morning.'

Michael took the button from her and examined it carefully. 'OK,' he said. 'But we'll get him a proper eye later, won't we?'

'We will, once I've had the baby and everything's settled down again. We'll sort it out.'

'And then next time we'll do a different kind of animal. A bird or something.'

'Oh, no,' said Nancy, teasing him. 'It's you who wants to be the taxidermist, not me.'

She ruffled his hair, and laughed.

'After this one,' she said, 'you're on your own.'

14

It's Saturday afternoon; Michael is at Phil and Kate's. Phil has had to go away for the weekend, on bank business. Michael wishes he'd known; he wouldn't have come.

He thumbs his way abstractedly through a magazine he found beside the settee, trying to pretend that he's alone, whilst opposite him Kate sits in an armchair, sewing name labels into a new school uniform.

A few long minutes pass, then, out of nowhere, Kate says: 'He envies you, you know.'

Michael keeps his eyes on the magazine. 'Who does?'

'Who do you think?'

He turns a page. 'I don't know.'

'Phil,' she says. 'Phil envies you.'

Michael looks up. Kate has paused in her sewing and is studying him intently, her arms folded, her face tight. She's looking at him in the same way that he'll look at one of his animals before he skins it, before the reconstruction begins. She's looking at, into, and beyond, his eyes. She's looking at the outside and the inside, looking and looking until the boundaries begin to blur, until the entire animal begins to emerge. Michael is suddenly aware of the fact that he's never been alone with her before, not for more than the odd few minutes. He returns to the magazine.

'Well?' says Kate.

Michael makes a small sound in his throat, part discomfort, part disbelief. 'I'm sure you're wrong,' he says.

'I don't think I am, Michael. There's envy there, and there's something else, too.'

Michael stiffens. 'I don't know what you're talking about.'

'I'm talking,' says Kate, 'about the fact that there's something wrong between you and my husband. Something unspoken. I can sense it, and I'd like to know what it is.'

'Why don't you ask Phil?' he says.

'Two reasons,' says Kate, flatly. 'First of all, he's forgotten how to talk. I mean really talk. He can move his mouth well enough, of course. God knows he can move his mouth. He could sell you a mortgage in his sleep. He could tell you more about money than you'd ever wish to know. But he could no more tell you what he's really feeling than fly to the moon.'

'Oh,' says Michael.

'And the other reason,' says Kate, 'is that, even if he wanted to give it, I'm not sure he has the answer.'

'And you think I have?'

'I don't know, Michael. You tell me.'

He lifts his face from the magazine and looks at her. Her attitude suddenly softens; her arms unfold, and her hands reach to her face, as if to smooth away the veneer, to bring back her real self. But the determination is still there in her eyes, and Michael can tell that he isn't going to get out of here without doing some talking.

'You've never really liked me, have you?' he says, slowly.

'That's not true,' says Kate. 'I don't even know you.'

'No, I suppose not. So –' He stops himself short.

'Yes?'

'Nothing.'

'Michael, I won't bite you, you know.'

'No,' says Michael. He can feel himself beginning to blush, like a little boy, like he's one of her kids, and he hates himself for it. 'Well, what I was going to say, actually, was, well, you say you don't know me, and that's true, you don't, but, having said that, what do you see? I mean, who do you think I am?'

'Do you want the truth, or something nice?'

For a moment, Michael's not sure whether or not she's being serious. But then she smiles.

'Can't I have a bit of both?' he says.

'Well,' says Kate, with mock gravity, 'I'll see what I can do.'

'Thanks.' Michael can't help himself – after all these years he's suddenly beginning to warm to her.

'So, let's start with some plus points, shall we?'

'Please.'

'OK. You're a very talented man, highly respected in your field. You're incredibly passionate about what you do – about nature, animals. Having that kind of passion, by the way, is what Phil envies you for.'

'I see.' Michael had already forgotten about Phil's envy.

'You're reasonably good-looking – though nothing special by Hollywood standards – and you work hard.'

Michael perceives a definite air of finality about his sister-in-law's last comment. 'Is that it?'

'Yes.'

'That's all the good points?'

'Yes.'

'And the bad points?' he says, wincing.

'You drink too much.'

'Ah.'

'And you're too wrapped up in your work. You've isolated yourself from the rest of the human race. You do what you do and it's your whole life and there's nothing else. My guess is you don't have a true friend in the world.'

'I have friends!'

'Name one. Name your closest friend.'

Michael thinks, but he's got to think quickly or it'll look as if she's right. He decides against mentioning any of the regulars from the pub, because Kate might know them herself and trip him up. In the end he says: 'Bob Sheldon.'

'Who's he?'

'He was one of my first proper customers. He found a dead owl by the side of the road and fell in love with it, brought it to me for preserving. He thought it was a barn owl. I said, "That's not a barn owl, it's a tawny." But as it happened there was a barn owl in the studio which I'd almost finished, and I showed him that. He fell in love with that one too, ended up buying them both. And when he came to pick them up we had another chat and he ordered a snowy owl. He'd got the bug, you see. He has two or three a year off me now; he must have one of the best owl collections in the country.'

'Right,' says Kate. 'And what does Bob do for a living?'

'He's a, er ... he's a businessman.'

'What sort of business?'

Michael is silent.

'Has he got any kids?'

'Yes!'

'How many?'

'Er –'

'What's his greatest wish?'

'Look,' says Michael, 'how on earth should I know what his greatest wish is? We don't talk about stuff like that. We ... '

Kate waits, quietly victorious.

'We ... '

She waits.

'We only ever talk about owls, all right? Happy now?'

There's a brief, strained silence before Kate begins to laugh. It's not an unpleasant laugh, not derisory. In fact, it's quite a nice laugh, a bit infectious, and Michael feels the corners of his mouth twitching against his will. He bites the inside of his bottom lip and tries to avoid looking at Kate, but he can't avoid her laughter, it's wheedling itself into his system and the muscles in his diaphragm are already beginning to bounce up and down with it. He bites harder on his lip and tenses his stomach, desperately trying to resist, but it's no good, he's beaten, and his mouth explodes open and suddenly they're both laughing together, feeding off each other. Soon they're laughing so hard they can barely breathe.

'Jesus,' says Kate, hugging her sides, 'I think I'm going to have a heart attack!'

'Please don't,' says Michael. 'I was hoping you'd make me something to eat!'

It's a good five minutes before they settle down again, and by the end of it Michael's glad he came, after all. It's funny, he thinks, how one little incident can have such a huge effect. Because in the midst of the unexpected laughter something important happened – Kate became his friend. Just like that. Only, he knows, it wasn't just like that at all. She forced it, she made the moment happen.

And she could have left it at that: two people connecting for the first time, deciding to like each other, to try and understand each other. A turning point, a genuine breakthrough. She could have left it at that, but she didn't. Because now she's got this line of communication open, there are more things she wants to know.

They've moved to the conservatory, a white PVC structure with a blue tiled floor and a big spider plant in the corner. Michael has just finished off his requested food, the kids have appeared, said hello, and disappeared again, and now Kate's asking about Nancy.

'What was she like? Do you remember?'

'What does it matter?' says Michael. 'What does it matter to you what Mum was like? Why do you want to know?'

'Because I'm married to her son, Michael. Because my children are her grandchildren. Because I'm ... interested.'

'Phil can tell you,' says Michael, his voice wavering slightly.

'But he won't,' says Kate. 'I can't get him to talk about her, I've tried. He's like your father, he just shuts it all out, thinks that because it's in the past it's over and done with.'

'And isn't it?'

'Oh, come on, Michael,' says Kate. 'I might not know you very well, but I know you better than that. You're not like those two, you haven't dulled your memory the way they have. You know that history never leaves us. Keeping the past alive is what you do for a living, for God's sake.'

'I preserve animals,' says Michael. 'That's all.'

'And what are they? What are these animals you preserve? Are they just so much material, nicely presented, or are they something more than that?'

Michael sighs. 'They're more than that.' He sighs again, more heavily, then he says: 'My mother was very ... beautiful.'

'Was she?' says Kate, softly.

'Yes. And I remember thinking, even when I was really young, that it couldn't be right that someone so beautiful should have to wear the same scruffy clothes all the time, and have to go out working in the fields and get mud in her hair. But no one else seemed to notice it, only me. And I still think life must have been so hard for her, what with the never-ending work, and the farmhouse falling down around us, and no one but Dad for company most of the time.'

'And was she unhappy, do you think?'

'Wouldn't you be?'

'I don't know,' says Kate, cautiously. 'I mean, she had you and Phil, didn't she? She had her children.'

'Yes,' says Michael. 'Yes, she had us. And she always found time for us, too, she always took us seriously. I don't remember her talking down to me, ever. If something was important to me, she'd let it stay important. Like ... like boredom.'

'Boredom?'

'When I was a kid, I'd get so bored sometimes that I just wanted to cry. Not often, but when it got me, it really got me. She found me lying on my bed once, emitting these pathetic little sobs, and when she asked me what the matter was, and I told her, she said, "Ah, boredom's a killer." And she sat me on her knee and told me

60

about how boredom used to get her too, when she was a little girl. How it used to creep up on her when she wasn't looking, and pounce on her from behind. She made it sound like a living thing, like an animal, or a monster. And I could see it that way, because that's how it felt, like something outside of myself, trying to make me miserable. She allowed it to be real, that's the thing.'

'Mmm,' says Kate, 'that's a nice memory. I know what my mum would have said.'

'So do I,' says Michael, 'and I've never even met her. She'd have done the obvious thing, she'd have reeled out a long list of possible things to do. I've even caught your Phil at it.' He mimics his brother's voice, in a tone that's halfway between parody and sarcasm. '"If you're that bored you can go and tidy your room – it looks like a bomb's gone off in there!" And when I hear him talk like that I think, Phil, have you forgotten?'

Kate shifts uneasily in her seat. Michael doesn't notice. He's slipped away again, back into the past. 'Mum used to take photographs. She once showed me some that she took of Calke Valley, before the flooding. Dad must still have them somewhere, I suppose.'

'Ah, yes,' says Kate. 'That's how she met him, isn't it, taking those photographs?'

There's a note of surprise in Michael's voice. 'How did you know that?'

'I'm not sure, now,' she says. 'I think maybe your Aunt Eileen mentioned it once.'

'Oh, Aunt Eileen.'

'Yes. In fact, she's the only member of your family I've ever got any reasonable details out of.'

Michael smiles vaguely. 'You're a real one for details, aren't you?'

'There's nothing wrong with that.'

'No,' says Michael. 'No, you're right. And as it happens Aunt Eileen was the only one who ever gave me any details when ... ' He drops his head slightly, runs a hand through his hair. 'You know,

Dad never said a word to us after it happened. I tried to talk to him, but he wouldn't give me anything.'

'Michael, I –'

'And I had so many questions. Questions about the baby. I wanted to know, was she alive when she was born? Was she alive for just a little while? And questions about Mum. I needed to know … I needed to know, did she –'

And the next thing Michael is aware of is that there is an arm around him. He can feel the gentle weight of it on his shoulders and he can hear Kate's voice telling him, 'Sshhh, sshhh, it's all right now.' His eyes are closed in grief and his breath is shuddering in his lungs. He's a nine-year-old boy whose Mum has just died.

'Sshhh,' says Kate. 'It's all right, Michael. I'm sorry. I'm really sorry, I shouldn't have brought all this up.'

'Why not? It was nearly thirty years ago. I'm a grown man, I ought to be able to talk about it.'

'But you never have, have you?' says Kate, letting go of his shoulders.

'No … No, not really.'

'Perhaps you should.'

'Yes,' says Michael. 'Perhaps I should.'

He lifts his head and takes a deep, deep breath, then lets it slowly out.

He says: 'You've never actually been in my studio, have you?'

'No,' says Kate. 'But I've seen some of your work. We went to Scarborough once, on holiday, and there was some of your stuff in the museum. And there was your exhibition of songbirds at the library a few years back – I saw that.'

Michael nods, not really hearing.

'In my studio, there's a pike. It was the first thing I ever did, and Mum helped me with it. It was a few weeks before she died. It's, er,' – he gives a strange little laugh, under his breath – 'well, it's a fairly odd-looking creation. It's two shades of bright green, with dabs of white here and there. We used a button off one of Mum's coats for an eye. It was only supposed to be temporary, until I could find out where to get a glass one, but it kind of grew on it. I mean, a real pike looks like a killer, hard and lean and deadly, and it needs a cold, hard eye. But my pike ... well, it's not the most accurate likeness I've ever achieved, and the button pretty much suits it.'

'It sounds quite something,' says Kate. 'I'll have to see it sometime.'

'No,' says Michael, shaking his head. 'I mean, it's not something for other people to look at, or laugh at, or whatever. It's' – he hesitates – 'it's my link to Mum. It's the thing that we shared, that I best remember. There's so much of my time with her that's gone, so many things we did that are lost to me forever. But whenever I'm in my studio, and I look up at the pike, it's like she's still here, with me. I can feel her presence.'

He falls into silence. He gets up off his seat and wanders over to the spider plant, absent-mindedly stroking its leaves.

'I even talk to her sometimes. It's ridiculous, isn't it?'

'No, Michael, it's not. Who's to say that she isn't watching over you?'

'Through the eye of a fish? An eye that isn't even an eye?'

Kate smiles gently. 'Does it matter how?'

Michael smiles too, despite himself. 'I suppose not,' he says.

15

Three days later, Kate is watering her garden when she hears the phone ring. There's no one in the house to answer it; Phil is at work and the kids are at school. She runs towards the back door, wiping her hands on her jeans as she goes. She doesn't want to miss this call. It's Michael, she knows it is.

She rushes in and grabs the receiver. 'Hello, Michael,' she says, breathless. 'How are you this morning?'

'I'm all right,' says Michael.

'Good. That's good.'

'Look, I'm feeling a bit embarrassed, Kate, but –'

'Don't be,' says Kate.

'No. Well. Anyway, I've been thinking about what you said on Saturday.'

'Oh?'

'About me and Phil.'

'Yes?'

'About what it is between us.'

'Yes?' She can feel him struggling on the other end of the line. 'Michael, would you prefer to pop over? There's only me here.'

'No, thanks. I just want to say that I can't forgive him, and I think that's the problem. I can't forgive him for not missing Mum.'

'But Michael,' says Kate, 'he does miss her. I'm sure he does, in his own way.'

'Well, that's it anyway. That's what I wanted to say.'

'OK, Michael. Well, er, thanks for ringing.'

'That's all right.'

'So we'll see you on Saturday, then?'

'Should do.'
'Right, then. Bye, Michael.'
'Bye, Kate.'

Call her. Pick up the phone, press a few buttons – how hard can it be? She left you her number – she deliberately left you her number. If she didn't want people phoning she wouldn't leave her number, would she?

So ring it.

Because you've got a question for her, haven't you?

Because you were just wondering if maybe ... That is, perhaps, would you like to, sometime, one evening maybe ... Jesus wept, you can't even get the rehearsal right – pull yourself together.

Now then, try again, nice and slowly:

Hello Clare ... (that's a good start – there's nothing wrong with that) ... this is Michael, Michael Marshall?...(ah yes, a hint of question in the voice, not too presumptive – very nice) ... The taxidermist? ...(just to be on the safe side).

Look, to get straight to the point, would you like to go out for a drink sometime?

Araneus Diadematus, the Garden Spider, sits motionless in the centre of his web, spun between a fence post and an abandoned plant pot in a corner of Michael's garden. He is an impressive specimen, almost half an inch long, with a distinctive white cross on his sandy brown abdomen. The last two hours of his life have been spent in meticulous construction, engineering the intricate network of threads that surround him, and now he waits for his reward. He can expect to do well – his is a well-proven method, perfected over tens of thousands of years, and any insect unfortunate enough to fly into his web should prepare to say goodbye to the world.

Any small insect, that is.

It is now July, and there are two dozen hornets living in the bird box – the queen, and twenty-three workers. The nest is, for the time being, a wholly feminine environment. The workers are always female; only later, when the summer is drawing to an end, will the males be produced to fertilise next year's queens.

The workers are already busy, collecting food for the next generation of larvae and for their queen, who in turn is busy laying yet more eggs. Although the workers themselves prefer sweeter foods, the larvae need protein, which comes largely in the form of other soft-bodied insects. The hornets, with their powerful limbs and crushing jaws, are well equipped to deal with these unfortunate creatures, which will include other, smaller, types of wasp. On capture, the hornets rapidly dismember their prey. Only the thorax, the middle section of the insect bearing the wings and legs, is deemed fit to be taken back to the nest.

Araneus Diadematus is not an insect, he is an arachnid. Nor does he have, strictly speaking, a thorax. But every rule has its exceptions, and Araneus Diadematus has the misfortune of being in the wrong place at the wrong time, with a body full of protein.

The hornets come and go with tireless persistence. Every few minutes one will enter the bird box with food, or leave it to find more. Their search takes them over an impressive area, and with each trip they extend their range, scanning the gardens of Michael's street, ten, eleven, twelve doors away. But always they fly in the same general direction, and always they pass over the spider's badly placed lair. It was only a matter of time before one of them spotted him, and now one has.

Araneus Diadematus holds himself absolutely still, as the hornet hovers in front of his web. Drifting slightly to the right, then a little to the left, as if in an effort to hypnotise, the hornet seems to know what she has to do. She must grasp the spider, and only the spider. She must avoid the treacherous netting.

A moment later it is done, efficiently and cleanly, and she alights on the ground nearby to complete her task. After the briefest of struggles, she bites Araneus Diadematus in half, discards his rear portion, and takes to the air with what is left of him firmly in her grip. His legs are still kicking. At the entrance to the bird box she pauses, making way for an emerging sister, before carrying him in.

18

'This place used to be a shop until a couple of years ago,' says Michael. 'An electrical shop, it sold tellies and things.' He's aware that it's not the most exciting statement ever to have passed his lips.

He and Clare are on their first date. He'd finally found the courage to make that phone call two days ago and she'd said yes, she'd love to go out for a drink with him. He'd quelled his nerves with a couple of cans of lager before coming out, and now they're sitting in a corner of the orange-walled spot-lit cube that is Curley's, Woodington's one and only wine bar. There are large black and white photographs of obese Italians on every wall. It's the first time that Michael has been in here and he doesn't like it one bit.

It appears that other people do though, because it's starting to fill up rapidly. Michael recognises some of the faces. He hadn't anticipated this. One of the reasons he'd chosen Curley's for tonight was that he thought it would be full of people he didn't know. That and the fact that he imagined Clare would feel more at home here than in The Roebuck or The White Horse or The Railway.

Most of the customers are men, and one of them, a small sweaty specimen in blue jeans and a red nylon shirt, is peering steadily over the top of his glass in the direction of Michael and Clare's table. Michael is trying to avoid making eye contact. He looks awkwardly up at the ceiling and hopes that Clare won't notice the staring man.

'Who's that?' asks Clare, casually. 'Looking at us?'

'Oh,' says Michael, 'that's Dodge. He's just someone who went to our school. People have always called him Dodge, I don't know why. I don't even know what his real name is.'

His real name, he thinks, *is nosey bloody bastard.*

Clare calmly directs her gaze towards Dodge, who suddenly finds the front of his shirt extremely interesting. 'So what's the fascination with us?' she says, smiling, allowing the thing to become a joke. 'Has he never seen you out with a woman before, or something?'

Before Michael can reply she lifts their empty glasses from the table and makes her way to the bar to order more. As she passes Dodge she slows and gives him another long, cool look. By the time she returns to Michael, Dodge has upped and gone.

'I meant to ask,' says Michael, when she's settled again at the table, 'how were your degree results? Did you get what you wanted?'

A brief look of disappointment crosses her face. 'Not really. I was hoping for a 2:1, but I just missed it.'

'Oh, that's a shame. Still, a 2:2's perfectly respectable, isn't it?'

'Respectable, yes.' She pauses, glancing over to the window as a trio of teenage girls appear then disappear beyond the glass. 'Just not anything special.'

'So, what are your plans now?'

'I don't know. I may take a bit of a break from studying for a while. There are one or two possibilities ...' She trails off, and it occurs to Michael that this is a discussion she'd rather not be having. She immediately confirms this by looking around the room with an expression of mock disdain and saying, 'Now then, are you going to show me some of this town's real pubs, or what?'

'Of course!' says Michael, pleased, and he drains his glass.

As they walk along the narrow pavement of Potter Street the conversation shifts to the subject of Michael's work. 'You know,' Clare says, 'I'd got a lot of preconceptions about taxidermy that had to go out of the window after I first spoke to you. I'd always thought it was a bit, well, creepy.'

Michael looks puzzled. 'Creepy?'

She gives an embarrassed little cough. 'I mean, on TV and in books it's always been portrayed as a bit ... macabre, hasn't it?'

Michael repeats the word slowly: 'Macabre.'

'But that's how a lot of people see it, isn't it?' says Clare – she struggles for a new way to put it – ' ... as a bit sinister.'

'Sinister.' There's a playful smile on the edge of his lips.

'That is,' she says, desperation creeping in, 'I thought, before I met you – and I'm sure a lot of people think this way – that there was something not altogether nice about the idea of having a dead animal hanging on your wall, that's all. I mean, in Cornwall, where Mum and Dad live, they've got the old country pubs, with display cases all over the place, a deer's head watching you drink your gin and tonic, and I couldn't even look at them without feeling, I don't know, guilty. I thought it was vulgar and inhumane to have them displayed like that. I thought taxidermy was a horrible practice, a disrespectful thing.'

'Oh,' says Michael.

'But I don't think that now!' she says, quickly. 'You made me rethink it all. Now I can see that people like you really love and understand those animals. It's like that crow, the one I did the sketches of? That day I first visited, I couldn't believe the way you spoke about it, how much you cared about it.'

'I think I was a bit drunk, actually,' says Michael.

'So?' says Clare, as they find themselves at the door of The Railway. 'What's that got to do with anything?'

She is just about to lead the way into the pub when she realizes that Michael is holding back. He stands on the threshold, smiling nervously, and asks: 'Would you like it?' He hesitates, feels himself reddening, but forces himself to finish. 'Would you like the crow ... as a present?'

'Pardon?'

'Would you like the crow, as a present?'

'Oh, Michael, I couldn't. Really, I couldn't.'

'No?'

'No, it's too much. Anyway, I seem to remember you saying you were going to keep it.'

'I've changed my mind,' says Michael. 'I always do, in the end. They're never good enough, I always look at them and know I could have done better. I never keep anything. I say I'm going to, but I don't.'

'Except for that pike above your freezer,' says Clare, lightly. 'That looks like it's been there a while.'

'Oh, that,' says Michael, and immediately, inside his head, he's back at the studio, standing in front of the freezer, with the pike before him. He looks at its eye, the button from his mother's blue coat. He sees – for the briefest of moments – his mother, in the onion shed, preparing onions for market, wearing that coat. The coat is splashed with mud and grime, and flecked with slivers of onion skin, and her hands and arms are red-raw with the cold, but she's smiling at Michael, smiling at her boy, and that smile lifts her up, and out of that dismal tin shack, and into the clear air of an eternal universe.

'That's different,' he says. 'Shall we go in now?'

19

The only two sure ways to avoid getting a hangover involve staying permanently sober, or permanently drunk. As far as Michael is concerned, neither of these options is particularly desirable, and this morning's hangover is a bad one. His head is pounding. His mouth is so dry that he can barely move his tongue. As he rises from his bed he feels his face beginning to sweat and burn, and his legs are close to buckling as he drags himself upright and makes his way into the bathroom.

He turns on the cold tap and thrusts his face into the flowing water, drawing what he can into his mouth with great gasps of relief, letting the remainder run over his cheek and down his neck. Then he turns the water off and straightens up to look in the mirror. His skin is pale, his eyes are bloodshot, and his hair is matted and straggly. His memory of last night is partial. Everything is as it should be, all things considered. It is cause and effect. He has woken in this state before, and he will wake in it again.

Over a scant breakfast of coffee and toast, he tries to remember the events of the night before. The earlier part of the evening he can recall well: meeting up with Clare in Curley's, that idiot Dodge gawping at them.

He can remember they talked about Clare's degree results, and about the public's perception of taxidermy. Clare seemed to have developed a real interest in his work. In fact – and Michael groans aloud as he considers this particular fact – he'd asked her if she'd like that carrion crow! Christ Almighty, what was he thinking? What kind of a man offers a girl a preserved crow on their first date?

He racks his brain for further details of the evening, searches inside himself for snippets of information. He remembers that, after Curley's, they had gone to The Railway for a swift one, and then on to The Roebuck, where they played pool, and she beat him three times on the trot. Or was it four?

He remembers Clare being amazed by The Roebuck's jukebox, which still plays the old vinyl singles. She said she'd never seen anything like it, it was like being in a time warp. Michael had put on his record – the record that was kept on the jukebox specifically at his request, the record that only ever got played by him. It was a strange, obscure Slade B-side, violin based, a sort of cross between a Thirties music hall song and an Irish jig. Clare thought it was truly terrible, and said so. The landlord overheard her, and agreed. An elderly man propped up at the bar overheard her, and agreed. A disembodied female voice, from somewhere over on the far side of the pub, agreed. Michael didn't care. He didn't care what people thought of his song, and neither, he suddenly realised, did he care whether or not people chose to pay attention to the fact that he was with a girl.

In fact, he had felt very at ease with her. The conversation flowed freely, and the awful silences that he had dreaded might occur, didn't. Clare had talked about her love of sport, particularly tennis, and her part-time work in a flower shop. She talked about her housemate, and best friend, Jaz, whom she described as a 'mad, but talented, painter'. She made passing references to her family – her parents in Cornwall, and an older brother out in Australia. She asked about his family, but only out of politeness, and he managed to deflect the questions and avoid talking about them.

He found plenty of other things to talk about, though, things he never even realised he was interested in. He talked about the way Woodington had changed since he was a child, how it had been transformed from a large but quiet village – a place where everyone knew everyone, or liked to think they did – to a steadily growing dormitory town for the city of Derby. How its farming and industry had undergone a continuous decline, with highly-priced housing estates starting to appear on the outskirts, on land that had originally grown crops, or grazed cattle, or where a textile mill or engineering works had once stood.

He told her what people had said about Curley's when it first opened. For weeks it had been a standard topic of conversation over a pint of bitter in The Roebuck, a double whisky in The White Horse. 'A poncey bloody wine bar, in Woodington! It'll never work. There's not the call for it, not here. It'll be shut within six months, I'm telling you.' But the doubters had all been wrong, because Woodington's new hidden population came out of their prestigious new houses, their converted barns, and adopted Curley's as their own. It was somewhere clean and arty, somewhere they weren't ashamed to take their friends from the city. And now, as Dodge had proved, even the locals were deciding to give it a try.

People had reacted in much the same way when the plans for a supermarket were announced, to be built on the site of the old timber yard. 'We don't need a supermarket,' they'd said, 'and we don't want one. Woodington's not big enough for a supermarket. There won't be enough trade, not for a bloody great place like that. It'll ruin the town centre. It'll close all our shops down, and then when they realise that there just aren't enough people here to keep it afloat, it'll shut. And where will we be then? Shopless. We'll have no greengrocer's, and no Co-op.' It was agreed by most, however, that Mick the Butcher stood a fair chance of survival, on account of his ability to make very old women feel like schoolgirls.

The supermarket's critics were half wrong, and half right. The greengrocer's shut immediately. The Co-op issued a statement saying that their rural policy was not based merely on profit, and that they were committed to a continued presence in Woodington, serving their loyal and valued customers. Then they shut, too. Mick the Butcher struggled on for several months, but it was only a matter of time before the 'To Let' sign was hanging outside his window, and the very old ladies of the town breathed a tired collective sigh. The supermarket thrived.

All of this, and plenty more besides, Michael had told Clare. He had talked and talked, and could tell that her keenness to listen was more than just good manners. She was, he sensed, genuinely enjoying his company. She liked him, and he liked her.

He liked her a lot.

20

The owl sits in its case in the showroom. The leaf has been refastened to the branch; there's no harm done.

'You've ... ' says Dennis, nodding towards the bird. Then he walks unsteadily back into the main part of the studio, sits himself down in a corner, and doesn't speak another word.

Michael is standing at his sink, washing a badger skin. It's work that requires no real concentration, that gives you time to think. Which is as well, because Michael's head is full of thoughts. *What's he doing here? This is his second visit in what, two months? He never visits.*

What's he doing here? Is it about last time, my little outburst? He's seen the bird, he knows it's all right now. It was only a leaf, for crying out loud.

What's he doing here?

What does he want?

After a long ten minutes of these thoughts Michael has had enough, and he decides to break the silence. He decides to ask his father ...

To ask him straight ...

If he'd like a cup of tea.

He opens his mouth to speak, but his father beats him to it because, 'Michael,' he says, 'I'm very ill.'

'Yes, Dad,' says Michael, working the badger skin between his fingers, gently massaging the last remaining knots of matted fur into submission. 'I know you are.'

'Won't be around ... forever.'

'No.' *OK, Dad, that's enough now. You can stop talking now.*

Dennis lifts himself from the chair, and clears his throat. 'Michael. Things I want ... to tell you. Things to say ... before –'

Michael shakes his head. *It's too late. Whatever you've got to say it's too late.*

'Michael –'

'Do you want a cup of tea?'

'Michael, please –'

'I'll make us some.'

Michael reaches over for the kettle, steadying himself against the sink. On the other side of the window a hornet – a newly emerged worker, returning from her first venture into the world, and plainly lost – is struggling with the concept of glass. What is this invisible barrier?

Michael hears his father's laboured breathing behind him, but his eyes remain on the hornet. That those slender, lacy wings can raise up that enormous barrel of a body is a miracle.

'Was stung once,' says Dennis. 'By one of them. At old farm ... when kid. Hell of a ... kick.'

'Well,' says Michael, his voice hard, 'you must have done something to deserve it. They're not aggressive.'

'Yes. Did something. Poked stick ... into nest. Then, ran. Only ... not quick enough.'

'There, then. You deserved it.'

And then something happens that takes Michael by surprise. His father speaks with a sudden desperate bitterness. He says: 'That's it? How life is? Get what we deserve?'

Michael has heard a lot of unhappy sounds come from his father's mouth over the years. He's heard the grumbling, the shouting, the odd curse. He's heard the endless coughing. But he's never heard anything like this. He turns away from the window and looks straight into his father's face, and just for a moment he sees it all – the anger, the fear, the courage, the shame ...

But still it's too late. He can't undo a lifetime of mistakes just like that, just because he's ...

Just because ...

'How bad is it? The emphysema?'

Dennis rests his back against the wall. 'Bad.'

'And what's going to happen?'

'Get worse. Only ... '

'What?'

'Can't get much worse. Lungs ... nearly done. Sooner or later –'

'But why are they getting worse? It's not like you still smoke, is it?'

Dennis drops his head, just enough to answer Michael's question.

'Oh, Dad. You stupid old sod. When did you start again?'

'Never stopped.'

'Oh, for God's sake!'

'Makes no difference now. Past that stage.'

'Yes, but still –'

'Still nothing,' he says firmly. 'My business. You don't say ... a word. Only telling you because –'

'What?'

'Because I'm trying to ... talk to you ... Michael. Properly. While still can.'

I know. I know you're trying.

Dennis gestures back towards the chair. 'Have to sit ... back down, Michael. Weary. Yes?'

'Yes, of course,' says Michael.

Dennis takes his seat again and Michael sits on the workbench, his legs gently swinging.

'So,' says Dennis. 'Hear you've been ... seeing young lady.'

'That's right,' says Michael. 'But it's only been a fortnight. So who told you?'

'Little bird.'

'It wasn't a waxwing was it?'

'Yes,' says Dennis. 'Flew ... from Scandinavia.'

They both grin through tight lips.

'A student?'

'Yes.'

'Bright, then?'

'Yes, Dad. A bright girl.'

'Good looker?'

'As it happens.'

'Tall blonde?'

'No, Dad. Average height, and dark.'

'Like your mother.'

Oh no. Oh God no. Now I see what you're doing.

'Michael, your mother ... '

Don't talk to me about Mum. Not now. Not after all these years.

'I ... '

I had so many questions. I was nine years old.

'I loved her, Michael. But, never did tell her. Never did say. Even when she was ... dying. Still never told her. Did it all wrong, Michael. Happened so fast. Couldn't think.'

This isn't happening. It's too late for all this, it's not happening.

'Haemorrhage. Can happen. Was very quick.'

Stop it.

'Don't know ... how much ... she knew. Do know she wasn't afraid. Not for herself.'

Stop it, stop it, stop it.

'Last thing she said ... "The baby?"'

Oh God. Oh God. My mother's last words.

'Should have said, "Baby's fine." Should have said, "You're going to be ... all right." Didn't. Couldn't. Couldn't do anything. Oh Michael, couldn't do anything.'

21

Michael and Clare are lying on twin sun loungers in Michael's back yard, the sun beating down on their closed eyelids. Two hours ago they had their lunch in The Blue Bell. They had a few drinks, then they came back and ended up making love on the floor of Michael's lounge. Now, though, the joy of it is already mingling in his mind with the recollection of Dennis's last visit.

It's not fair, the way this business with his father is overshadowing things. He's in love with Clare, and part of him desperately wants to tell her all about himself. But everything he has to say links inevitably back to his childhood, back to his family, back to the things he can't talk to her about, not yet. And she's started to notice. Over their last two or three dates she's been digging for information, and he's been resisting, and it's going to become a problem.

It's her housemate Jaz's birthday next week, and they're having a party at the house. Clare's suggested that he brings Phil along, but he hasn't passed the invitation on. He can't risk anything that might let her get a glimpse of what a mess he is inside. It could ruin everything.

With Kate, somehow, it's different. He can talk to her. But, then, she's his sister-in-law, not his girlfriend. He doesn't have to worry about scaring her off, and since his little breakdown at her house she already knows how screwed up he is anyway. He bumped into her the other day, outside the supermarket, and they ended up sitting in the park, chatting for the best part of an hour.

Mostly they had talked about Clare – it was good to be able to discuss her with someone and Kate had seemed really pleased for him. The whole conversation had left him with a good feeling inside. There'd been no talk of family this time. Of Phil, or his Mum, or Dennis.

Dennis. He's been thinking about him almost constantly since that day at the studio. He's been trying to come to terms with the fact that the inside of his father's head is a place he's never known, a secret that his eyes have never betrayed. He's been summoning up images of him, pictures of those times when he most needed to know the landscape that was hidden behind those distant eyes, behind the frowns, the occasional smile.

The night after Michael's tenth birthday, Dennis had walked up to the Woodington Arms. It was the first night he left the boys alone in the house. He had checked on them to make sure they were asleep, but Michael had fooled him. He heard his father go, and he heard him return, the heels of his heavy boots scuffing the loose grit at the far end of the drive. Peering through the corner of his bedroom window, Michael saw a tiny red dot glow and fade, glow and then fade, which was his father, smoking.

Which was his father, thinking.

About what?

Now Michael's father is ploughing the Big Field, the broad strip of land that climbs the gentle slope of the remaining valley. The freshly turned earth lies dark against the rest of the ground which still holds remnants of the morning's frost. He's approaching the top of the field, in a tractor that is in essence a Massey Ferguson Sixty-five, though it carries a visible history of adaptation and improvisation. The huge red cab once belonged to a larger tractor, as did the oversized mudguards that rattle and shake as if in fear of the engine's crude power.

Michael stands unseen at the bottom of the field. He's holding a flask of tea for his father, complete with a small plastic bowl for Sheba. Sheba is Michael's sheepdog. No, Sheba *was* Michael's sheepdog. Now she is his father's dog, she has adopted him. She goes with him everywhere. They are friends, they know each other. Michael watches them, side by side in the cab, two silhouettes removed and protected from the world by this glass and metal box.

The tractor turns, the plough raised above the earth like a huge steel hand, before the shares are lowered once more and it begins its steady descent to the bottom of the field. Above the straining engine, man and dog are enclosed in a shared solitude, in complete absorption and peace. It's a peace that Michael does not want to disturb. And it's a peace that he wants to enter. He wants to run to the tractor, bang his fists on the door of the cab and say, 'Father, let me in.' But he doesn't. He stands and waits with the tea until the image is shattered by Clare's quiet words.

'I could lie here forever,' she murmurs.

Michael's eyes snap open and he's back in the here and now. 'Mmm?'

'I said, I could lie here forever. It's wonderful, isn't it, just to stop, and lie in the sun, and appreciate what a fabulous thing it is to be alive.'

'I suppose it is,' says Michael. 'Not that we always have the sun to lie in, mind.'

'No, that's true.' She pauses for a moment, then says, 'I had a letter from our James yesterday – it's almost seventy degrees where he is. And it's winter there.'

Michael says nothing, so she continues: 'It gets well over a hundred in the summer. The record's almost a hundred and twenty.'

'Now that is hot.'

'He says you get used to it.'

'I'm sure.'

They both fall silent for a moment.

'I miss him a lot, you know. I miss having him near.'

'Yes,' says Michael, quietly.

Then, suddenly, Clare props herself up on her elbows and peers down at the stretch of garden between the yard and Michael's studio. 'You know,' she says, 'I'd have thought that someone who loves nature the way you do might have been a better gardener.'

Michael sits up on his lounger, and pretends to be offended. 'And what exactly is wrong with this garden?'

'Those, for a start,' she says, pointing to a large cluster of nettles.

He emits an exaggerated snort. 'They're as much a part of nature as anything else, aren't they?'

'Maybe they are,' says Clare, swinging her legs off the lounger, 'but if I can find a pair of gloves they're coming out!'

'I thought you said you could –'

'Never mind that, I want to do some gardening.'

'Right,' says Michael, 'I'll, er, get some gloves then.'

'Two pairs,' she says. 'You're helping.'

'Right,' says Michael.

'You don't really want any of these weeds, do you?' she says later, as she works her finger around a particularly stubborn dandelion root.

Michael is crouched beside her. 'No,' he says, 'of course not. We can pretty much clear everything, except for that.' He points to a gangly white buddleia, the result of a stray seed that managed to set itself a couple of years ago. 'I don't think the hornets would forgive me if I got rid of that. They're quite fond of it.'

Even as he speaks, one of the hornets alights on the plant, and the front half of its body disappears amongst the flowers.

Watching, Clare fails to hide a faint shudder. 'You know,' she says, 'I appreciate the way you feel about those things. And you've told me that they aren't aggressive, and of course I believe you. But I can't for the life of me feel comfortable when they're so close.'

'Well, that's understandable,' says Michael. 'I mean, I accept that they don't look particularly friendly, but they really won't hurt you.

Anyway, they'll be gone come winter. When the frosts start, the whole nest will die out.'

'They don't just go on, then, like honey bees?'

'No, no. They'll produce a few new queens towards the end of the season, and a handful of males to fertilise them, then the queens will go off and overwinter somewhere. Then next spring, if they're lucky, they'll wake up, find a good place for a nest, and start again.'

'And if they can't find a good place they'll come back to your bird box.'

'No, again. They'll start from scratch. They never reuse an old nest.'

Clare looks decidedly pleased as she gets back to her dandelion.

'Good,' she says.

22

It's a forty minute bus journey from Woodington to Derby, which gives Michael plenty of time to feel anxious. He's wearing his usual jeans, tee shirt and jacket and he wonders if he should have put on something a little smarter. He's not used to thinking about clothes. He's not used to going to parties.

Michael hasn't been to the house before. Up until now Clare has always come over to Woodington. He hasn't met any of Clare's friends yet, either, and he knows that he's going to be under scrutiny. There'll be Jaz, of course, and others too, from the university, from the tennis club. And Michael knows – he just knows – that they'll all be outgoing and trendy and young, and they'll all be trying to work out what exactly it is that Clare sees in him.

Reaching down, he lifts a can of beer from the carrier bag sitting between his ankles, opens it up, and takes a swig. It won't hurt to get one or two down before he arrives. There are plenty more in the bag.

When he reaches the bus station, Clare is waiting to meet him. She's wearing a neat, dark suit and she's had her hair trimmed into a tight bob. As he steps off the bus she smiles at him, then looks past him, obviously hoping to see Phil.

The disappointment shows in her face when she realises he's alone. 'Couldn't your brother make it?'

'No,' says Michael, not quite looking at her. 'He's, er, not very well.'

'Pity,' she says, 'I'd like to have met him. I haven't met any of your family yet.'

'I've not met yours, either.'

'Yes, but mine aren't exactly on our doorstep, are they?'

'No, well, another time, eh?'

'Yes,' she says, her smile returning. 'Yes, of course.'

'I like your hair, by the way.'

'Do you really? I'm not sure.'

'I think you look great.'

'Thanks,' she says, and they begin the walk towards the house.

She leads him through the city streets, giving him a quick run-through of some of the people who will be at the party. 'You'll like Jaz,' she says, 'I promise. And her crowd are all right, on the whole. There are one or two that can be a bit pretentious, but they're OK once you've got used to them.' She hesitates slightly, then continues: 'You might want to try and avoid her brother Andrew, though. He's a bit of a hard-line animal rights campaigner, and somehow I don't think you two would hit it off.'

'Right.'

'It's just, he's a bit provocative.' She hesitates, her thoughts elsewhere, then she says, 'Anyway, there'll be plenty of other people to talk to. And some of my friends will be there, too, don't forget – I can't wait for you to meet them!'

'Yes,' says Michael, 'it'll be ... nice,' and he smiles weakly.

Once there, Clare is soon busying herself, mingling with the guests, seeing to the music, bringing out more food. Although it's Jaz's party, she seems to have taken on the role of host. Every now and again she glances over her shoulder in Michael's direction, to make sure that he's not feeling stranded. Whenever Michael catches her eye he responds with a reassuring smile. It's genuine, he's actually finding the whole thing quite enjoyable. Maybe it's just the beer he had earlier, or the red wine that one of Clare's tennis friends keeps topping him up with, but he feels much less out on a limb than he'd thought he would.

The house is bigger than he expected. It's got two lounges, and the one he's in now must be twice the size of his at home. The rent for a house this size in Woodington would be a small fortune.

He casts his eyes around the room and spots a wiry-looking youth standing in the far corner. He knows immediately that it's Andrew, the animal rights activist. Even from this distance, there's a distinct suggestion of suppressed violence about him. He's in conversation with a girl sitting on the sofa to his right, but instead of lowering his head to speak to her, he keeps it high, and lowers his eyes. His right hand holds a cigarette. His left is flattened against the wall, at waist height.

Michael tries not to pay too much attention to the youth. He tries to tell himself that Clare was right – this is Jaz's night, and if this Andrew is a bit of an extreme type, then perhaps it's best that they don't meet. But then again, Michael would quite like the opportunity to explain that he, too, is someone who loves animals. That much, however they choose to frame things, is something they have in common.

Clare's friend is still intent on plying Michael with red wine, and Michael is not refusing. The two are having a light, meandering conversation, skipping across the surface of a variety of harmless topics. Twice the friend has tried to introduce the subject of golf, but Michael has managed to divert them on to football, which he can summon at least some enthusiasm for. It's not the sort of conversation he would normally find himself involved in but, considering his earlier feelings of trepidation about coming to the party, he can live with it.

It occurs to Michael that the friend is also pleased to have found someone to talk to, as if he too had been dreading the party. He's not the gregarious, inquisitive, confident kind of person that he had expected to be confronted with, and he feels a certain empathy towards him. When he begins his third attempt at introducing golf into the conversation, though, Michael realises that enough is enough. He announces that he's going to go and join Clare, who he can see has taken a break from her hosting duties to join a conspiratorial huddle of women in the hallway.

'Well, I was thinking of moving on anyway,' says the friend, unconvincingly. 'Nice meeting you.' And he goes off to find his coat.

Michael makes his way across the room but he gets barely halfway before a very intoxicated Jaz appears from nowhere, throws her arms around him, and shuffles him into another corner. 'Michael!' she says, loudly. 'We meet at last! I've heard so much about you!'

Michael is by now drunk enough not to be too embarrassed by this unexpected display of affection, but he's nevertheless a bit taken aback. 'Er, hello,' he says.

'Your glass!' she screams, in reply. 'It's empty! It's my birthday and your glass is empty!'

'Er, yes,' says Michael. 'But only just.'

'Only just? Only just! How can a glass be only just empty?'

'Well –'

'No, no!' she says, stopping him before he starts. 'It all makes perfect sense, my dear.' She lets go of his neck, takes a step back and lifts up her arms in a theatrical gesture, as if about to deliver some profound and constant truth. 'There are, we are told, two kinds of people in this world. There are those for whom the glass is half full, and those people we call the optimists, the positive thinkers, who will imagine us into a better world. And, of course, of course, let us not forget, there are those others ... the, er ... '

'The half empties?' offers Michael.

'The half empties! The half empties! Who are the pessimists, although they will tell you they are merely the realists, although I will tell you –' she leans towards him, in confidence '– that they are merely the miserable bastards!' She nods her head, sagely, satisfied with her analysis, before remembering the point she had started out to make. 'Oh, yes,' she says. 'We are told that there are these two kinds of people, but we are told wrongly, that is, we are deceived, that is, there is another kind of person in this world. Because there is people like you, Michael. People for whom the glass is only just empty!'

Michael looks at her in silence, waiting to make sure that she's finished. 'All I meant,' he says, 'is –'

'I know what you meant,' says Jaz. 'You meant it was time for another. Bloody good idea, come on,' and she thrusts her arm through his and drags him off towards the kitchen. 'Red wine,' she says, 'it's fantastic! Makes your teeth go all black of course, but ... Show us your teeth, Michael! Show us your teeth!'

Michael scans the room in semi-alarm as Jaz pulls him across it, and as they pass the hallway door he sends a mock plea for help in Clare's direction. Clare just laughs.

Despite its current status as some kind of shrine to alcohol, the kitchen – or as much of it as can be seen beneath the cans and glasses and bottles – seems to Michael to have that distinctly welcoming feel that a single man's kitchen can never quite achieve. It's a spacious, calm room, with clean, wood-fronted units and a number of small abstract paintings on the pale yellow walls. The paintings, which he guesses to be Jaz's creations, are particularly good as abstracts go. With their flowing lines and mellow shades they add to the warmth and subtlety of the room, they're part of what gives it its peace. He can imagine, on quieter evenings, Jaz and Clare sitting around the pine table, cradling mugs of coffee and discussing their lives.

In the corner of the kitchen, perched precariously on the worktop next to the microwave, is a comatose young man, not much more than a boy. His eyes are closed beneath a long fringe of dark hair and his thin arms are wrapped around an acoustic guitar. He's clinging on to it as if it's all he has in the world.

Jaz gives the boy a shake. 'Anyone in there?'

The boy comes to, peering around him as if he's wakened into someone else's reality. 'What's up?' he says.

'Know any Elvis?'

'No.'

'All right, back to sleep,' says Jaz, and she starts rooting through the wine bottles on the table, looking for one that meets her approval. In a second, the boy is back in his dreams.

'I take it you're an Elvis fan,' says Michael.

Jaz answers by launching into a particularly earthy version of *Always on my Mind,* while she pours the wine into two half pint glasses, before thrusting one into his hand. 'So tell me,' she says, as if the thought has just occurred to her, 'how are you enjoying my party?'

'It's very nice,' says Michael.

'Nice?'

'I mean, great. It's fine. I'm having a good time. Honestly.'

She begins to giggle. 'It's all right,' she says, 'you don't have to go overboard.'

'No,' says Michael.

'So, then, who have you met? I saw you were talking to Craig.' She giggles again. 'I bet that was exciting.'

'He was OK,' says Michael.

'Did he talk about golf?'

'He tried.'

'And that's OK, is it?'

'It's not the end of the world.'

'Well, bless you!' says Jaz. 'You're very tolerant. Anyway, he's gone now so we're all safe. So who else have you met? Have you met Rubens, the archaeologist? Tall, thin, bald head, glasses? Now he is an interesting chap – you'll get no golf out of him.'

'Well, to be honest, I've hardly met anyone except for Craig,' says Michael. 'But I'm not bothered. I'm not one of life's most sociable people anyway. I tend to sit on the edges and watch, if you know what I mean.'

Jaz nods with exaggerated gravity. 'You're an observer.'

'That's right. It's part of my job to observe, to catch the details.'

'Ah yes, your job,' she says. 'Which brings me to another matter. Brother Andrew. I take it you've not met him, then?'

'No,' says Michael, 'but Clare –' and he just manages to stop himself saying that Clare had 'warned him off'. 'Clare's told me about him.'

'Has she?' Jaz sounds surprised. 'I got the impression she hadn't.'

'Well she has,' says Michael.

'Oh. Still, there's no reason why not.'

'That's right. We're all entitled to our opinions.'

'Although –' says Jaz, but before she can finish, and as if summoned, Andrew stalks in through the kitchen door.

Michael tries to catch Andrew's eye but he won't look in his direction. Instead he nods towards the guitar boy in the corner and says to Jaz, 'I see Miles is pissed again.'

'Yes,' says Jaz, quietly. She seems apprehensive, suddenly sober.

Andrew opens the fridge and reaches in for a bottle of beer. Michael coughs, trying to get his attention. He's almost close enough to touch but still he hasn't acknowledged him. Andrew's got the beer, and he's about to leave again, when Michael decides that he's not going to let him go. He steps sideways in front of him, smiles, and extends his hand. 'Hi, I'm Michael,' he says. 'Clare's –'

Andrew freezes before him. 'I know who you are,' he says, ignoring the proffered hand. He's got a cold voice and that same aloof look about him that Michael had noticed earlier. He smiles, a thin, humourless smile. 'And I know what you are, too.'

'And what's that?' says Michael, taken aback.

Andrew is about to answer when Jaz cuts in. 'Andrew,' she says, with force, 'you've got your drink, now leave us alone, please.'

'Oh,' says Andrew, his voice heavy with sarcasm, 'but our friend seems to require some –'

'This is my house! Leave this kitchen now, or you can get out altogether.'

Andrew raises his arms in surrender. 'OK, Sis, OK. It's your party. Perhaps I can catch up with Michael some other time.' He brushes past Michael, with a look of utter contempt on his face. 'After all,' he calls back, over his shoulder, 'I know where he lives.'

The moment he's gone, Jaz begins apologising. 'I'm so sorry about that,' she says. She looks genuinely hurt, as if the slight had been as much against her as Michael. 'He's not normally that aggressive.'

'Just sometimes?' says Michael, still a little stunned.

'Well, yes, in truth. But it's like they say, you can't choose your relatives. And his heart's in the right place, usually.'

'Is it? I have to say I'm not convinced. That "I know where you live" line sounded like some sort of threat to me.'

'Oh, don't worry about that. He's still not come to terms with Clare finishing with him, that's all. He wouldn't exactly be over the moon about you, whoever you were.'

'Oh, I see,' says Michael, suddenly understanding, and trying desperately hard to conceal his surprise.

He fails miserably, Jaz isn't fooled. 'You didn't know, did you? About them?'

'No,' says Michael, 'I didn't know that they were … ' Suddenly there's an image in his head, which he tries to shake off, tries to rid himself of, but he can't. Clare and this idiot. Clare and this despicable, sneering … The two of them …

'Michael?'

He snaps to. 'Sorry,' he says, shaking his head, blinking the vision away.

'You said that Clare had told you.'

'That he was an animal rights activist. A bit provocative. Not that they were –'

He stops himself, stops the image from coming back. It's nothing. It shouldn't matter. But there's something about this Andrew, something really ...

'I'll tell you what,' says Jaz, 'I wish none of it had happened in the first place. It put me in a terrible situation when it started going wrong. You know, with being the sister and the best friend, always stuck in the middle. It was awful. And then when Clare finished it, he'd be coming round, pretending to visit me, when really he wanted to talk to her. He only lives up the road – he's got a flat above the newsagent's – and he'd be here two, three times a day some days. I mean, Clare's wonderful, I love her, I really do, and I can see how it must have hurt him when they split, but he's got to let her go ... '

She looks into Michael's disappointed face. 'I really wouldn't worry about it,' she says. 'It's history. And Andrew's just sore, still, that's why he was so horrible. If I know him, he'll have got his coat by now and gone off home in a huff. Let's get these glasses topped up and get back into it, shall we?'

'In a minute,' says Michael, brooding. 'But first, if you don't mind, can I ask you something?'

'Of course.'

'What ... ' He falters, annoyed with himself for having to ask, for needing to know. 'What do you think she saw in him?'

'That's easy,' says Jaz. 'Passion.'

'Right,' says Michael, wretched. 'Thank you.'

'It's what she sees in you, too, if you want to know.'

'Right,' says Michael. But he doesn't feel passionate any more. He feels let down by Clare, and it's all the worse because he knows she's done nothing wrong. He drops his head sorrowfully, and stares at his feet. All the fun's gone out of the party.

23

Gypsy is frantic with worry because her master won't get up. He is lying, twisted, at the foot of the stairs, making strange gasping noises. His eyes are closed. She has tried to bring him round, but her efforts have been in vain. When she tugged at the cuff of his jacket sleeve it was like trying to move a dead man. When she licked at his forehead she got no response, just an unnatural heat beneath her tongue. There is nothing more she can do.

She dashes away, noses open the door of the downstairs loo, jumps up onto the cistern, then scrambles onto the window ledge. She stands up on her back legs, hooks her front paws over the centre rail of the open window and launches herself into the daylight. It's not the first time she's performed this trick, but she's never done it so fast.

24

In taxidermy, as in most crafts, the secret of success lies largely in the preparation, and the correct handling of skins is essential. Once removed from the flesh, they must be cleaned thoroughly, and dried with care. The process varies depending on the type of animal. Mammal skins require tanning, destroying the microscopic bacteria that might otherwise, over time, attack their fabric. Michael tans his mammal skins using the traditional method, soaking them for many hours – or days, even – in a large vat of salt alum.

Bird skins are more straightforward. These he washes in the sink, using nothing more than a household detergent, after which he dries them off with a hairdryer. This is what he is doing when Gypsy arrives, and because of the noise of the hairdryer it's a little while before he hears her desperate whining coming from the other side of his door. When he finally opens the door she rockets into the studio and leaps up at him repeatedly, emitting wild yelps.

Michael can see that she's exhausted. 'Hey, slow down!' he says. He lifts her up into his arms, trying to calm her, as he steps out into the yard to look for his father. Dennis isn't there.

Michael holds the little dog out in front of him, his hands hooked under her front legs, and looks into her face. 'What's the matter?' he says.

Her eyes give him the answer and a moment later he's grabbed a coat, locked up the studio, and they're both running to Dennis's house in Alma Street. 'This is like something from *Lassie,*' he says to himself, and he regrets the words as soon as they come out. Because this isn't funny.

At Alma Street Michael finds both doors locked and no answer to his furious knocking. He dives into the neighbours' house, tells them to phone for an ambulance, and returns to set about breaking the lock on his father's back door. The man from two houses up is out in his garden and, seeing Michael, comes over to help. Between them they break open the door and Michael rushes in. Gypsy is already with her master, trying once more to revive him.

Within five minutes, the ambulance has arrived.

25

Dennis is lying in one of four beds in a High Dependency Unit in the Queen's Medical Centre, Nottingham. He has two broken ribs from the fall. On one side of him a cardiac monitor screen blinks and beeps quietly to itself, on the other side two small pump units – propelling saline and morphine through narrow plastic tubes into a vein in his arm – whirr away almost inaudibly. Above him a larger tube emerges from a hole in the wall, connecting to a mask that covers his nose and mouth. This tube is delivering pure oxygen.

The broken ribs, in conjunction with his advanced emphysema and now his immobility, mean that an infection is practically inevitable. It is already establishing itself, and Dennis is in no condition to stave off this further attack. His years of illness have worn him down; because his lungs have been unable to deliver sufficient amounts of oxygen into the bloodstream, his whole body has suffered. His heart, which must work so much harder when every breath is an effort, struggles to cope with a perpetually low supply of air. His immune system is tired and undernourished, using up all of its resources just to keep the body going. It finds it difficult to defend the body against even the most minor of ailments. It cannot cope with an infection.

Dennis is either unconscious or asleep, Michael's not sure which. Although they've been in the hospital for almost nine hours – it's now almost midnight – he hasn't been able to get any clear information about his father's state. There's a nurse on permanent duty in the unit, and she comes to check on Dennis every hour or so, ticking off little boxes on his observation charts, but she's no help to Michael.

He asks her, for the second time: 'Is he going to be OK?'

She avoids his eyes, and says: 'I'll get the doctor to speak to you as soon as he can.'

'But we've been here since three o'clock this afternoon! When's this doctor coming?'

'I don't know, Mr Marshall – as soon as he's free,' says the nurse. Then she yields a little, and says: 'Look, we're doing everything we can for your father, but these things can be complicated. It really is best that you wait until the doctor is able to go through it with you properly.'

That's what she said last time he asked. Whatever she knows – and she must know something – she isn't letting on.

'Why don't you go home and have some rest?' she says. 'I could get the doctor to phone you.'

'I'd rather stay,' says Michael. 'For a while.'

Two hours later nothing has changed, except that Michael has started to feel increasingly uncomfortable about the fact that he hasn't yet contacted anyone to tell them what's happened. He should have phoned Kate and Phil by now. Aunt Eileen, he should have phoned her. Perhaps Clare, too.

He tries to convince himself that he hasn't phoned because he hasn't got anything firm to report about Dennis until he's talked to the consultant. He tells himself that everything is being done that can be done, that having a selection of worried people around the bed isn't going to do anyone any good. It's rubbish, though, and he knows it. The real reason he hasn't phoned is because today has been the first time since he was a very small child that he's been able to spend any amount of time with his father without feeling that confusion of resentment and fear and hopelessness that's always there between them, that burns away inside him, that can't find a voice, that can't find peace. It's the first time for years that he has been in a room with him without wishing that he would go away and leave him alone.

He looks at the frail, broken man lying before him. Once Dennis had the power of a horse. He lived to work, and the work made him strong. Now his limbs are thinned, his muscles wasted. Perhaps now, as Michael senses the physical presence of his father more intensely than ever before, he will get what he wanted all those years. Maybe Dennis's eyes will never open again. Maybe he's wished him away forever.

26

There's a storm on the way. The first swollen drops of rain are crashing onto the glass of Michael's kitchen window.

'She's going to be a big one,' he says.

Clare isn't listening. She's looking through an expensive, trashy, women's lifestyle magazine, and tutting at its general dreadfulness.

She glances up. 'Sorry?'

'The storm,' says Michael, peering out at the darkening sky. 'She's going to be a big one.'

'Oh,' says Clare, absently. 'Oh ... yes.'

She goes back to examining the magazine.

Then she stops. And looks up again. And says, 'Why *she*?'

Michael looks at her blankly.

'What makes this storm a *she*?'

'Oh,' says Michael, 'I've always thought of storms as female ...' – he turns back towards the window, making the words slowly, giving himself time to think – ' ... I suppose it's because they've got that almost mystical combination of grace and power that could only ever be female.'

He continues to look out of the window, avoiding her eyes. He feels fairly sure that he's got away with it.

'You're full of it,' says Clare.

She puts the magazine down, joins him at the window, and they're both gazing out into the darkness as she slips her hand into his. He squeezes her fingers ever so slightly. She doesn't squeeze back. She allows her hand to be held.

There's a flash of lightning in the far distance, briefly illuminating the world outside.

'I'm sorry about your Dad,' she says, quietly.

There's a short silence, then the first low rumblings of a roll of thunder.

'How bad is it?'

Michael doesn't speak. He looks out into the night. He knows that this is a big moment, he knows what is happening. He is being offered the chance, and the challenge, of sharing his life. What was it Kate had said that time? *You've isolated yourself.* Kate was right, he knows that. Now he's being asked to come out of isolation – it's part of the deal. But he doesn't know if he can.

'Michael, will you talk to me please?'

'It's bad,' says Michael, tersely.

'I see,' she says, and he feels the slightest movement of her hand in his.

A little voice deep inside of Michael begins to wail. *Please don't pull away. Please let me hold your hand. I'll talk.* But Clare can't hear the little buried voice. She needs to hear the voice of a man.

He speaks in little more than a whisper. 'I'm scared.'

'That he's going to die?'

'No, it's not that.'

'Then what, Michael?'

'It's everything.'

'Then why don't you tell me about it?'

'Because so much of it makes no sense. Because I don't understand it myself. I've got so many things going around in my head and I can't bring any order to them. All these thoughts and feelings are bubbling away and I can't pull them into focus, I don't know how to put them into words.'

'Well maybe that's just lack of practise. But it doesn't mean you've got to stay that way forever, Michael. It doesn't mean you've got to shut me out.'

There's a marked bitterness in the tone of Clare's voice that makes him redden with shame.

'Is that how it feels? Like I'm shutting you out?'

'Of course it is, I'm only human. We've been going out for almost two months now, and every time I've mentioned your family you've either gone diving off into some completely unrelated subject or you've just clammed up altogether. How do you expect me to feel?' She pauses, then she says, 'I never planned any of this, you know. I wasn't looking for any of this.'

Michael turns to face her. 'What do you mean?'

'I mean,' she says, 'that I didn't wake up one morning and decide, "I know, I think I'll embark upon a relationship with an incommunicative alcoholic taxidermist fifteen years older than I am, today." That's all.'

He stares at her in surprise. 'Does it bother you, then, that I have a drink or two?'

'You don't have a drink or two, Michael. You're pissed every night.'

'And you don't like that?'

'Not much, no.'

'And the age difference, that bothers you too?'

'That doesn't matter, you're not exactly a pensioner. Anyway, you're as old as you feel, aren't you?'

Michael looks forlornly down at the floor. 'Do you know how old I feel?' he says.

'Tell me,' says Clare.

'You really want to know?'

'Yes.'

He hesitates. 'Well, there are two answers to that question. When I'm working, when I'm with my animals, or talking about my animals, I feel the age I am, I feel like a man in his late thirties. I feel it because I know I've got thirty-odd years of knowledge and experience behind me. I know my subject, I know my craft, better than most. When it comes to taxidermy, I have the skills ... '

He falls silent.

'And the other answer?' asks Clare.

'The other answer is the hard one.'

'But I want to hear it.'

'I know you do.'

She looks at him expectantly. 'So?'

'Well, the other answer is to do with relationships, intimacy. That's when my problems start. I can tell you precisely how old I feel then. I feel nine years old, Clare. Like a little boy, lost and out of my depth. If you could have seen the torment I put myself through, just plucking up the courage to ask you out, you'd have laughed.'

'I wouldn't,' says Clare, smiling. 'Actually, I think it's rather sweet.'

'That's because you don't understand what I'm saying,' says Michael, more abruptly than he intended. 'I'm not just talking about having a few nerves. It's more than that. I only phoned you in the end because I couldn't not, because the pain of not seeing you again was worse than the pain of making the call.'

'I still think it's sweet,' says Clare, ignoring the sharpness of his tone.

'But it's not just to do with women. It's with me everywhere, this feeling that people are almost another species, that I'll never truly understand them.'

'The way you understand your animals?'

'Yes.'

'I see. And has it ever occurred to you that your passion for animals is maybe your way of avoiding having to place your trust in people?'

At this question, Michael looks directly at her, his eyes meeting hers.

She says: 'Why nine years old, Michael? You said you could tell me exactly how old you feel at times ... ' – she gives a tiny wry smile – ' ... at times like this. And you said nine years old.'

Michael doesn't reply. He just gazes at her, through her.

She speaks again, slowly, carefully. 'Did something happen to you, when you were nine? Did someone do something to you? Michael?'

When Michael realises what Clare is suggesting, he snaps back to his senses. 'God, no!' he says. 'It was nothing like that.'

'So what the hell was it?' she says, finally losing her patience.

It comes out in a continuous half-shouted torrent. 'It was my mother, OK? I was nine when she died, and I've never got past it, I've never got past losing her. I know that it's no good, I know that it's not normal, but it's there all the time. The pain is there, all the time. All this business with my Dad at the moment just makes it worse, because I blame him. I shouldn't but I do. Half of the feelings I have every day of every week are feelings that I shouldn't have, but I do. Like when I was at your house, at Jaz's party, she told me about you and Andrew, and the moment she did, I was torn up with jealousy. I felt it eating away inside of me like acid. I felt angry towards you, as if you'd deliberately done something to hurt me. It's been playing on my mind ever since, swimming around in there with all the other madness. There's no logic to me feeling like that, there's no reason why I should care what you did before you met me, or who you did it with. But logic and reason don't count with me, do they, because I'm fucking crazy, aren't I? There, is that what you wanted to hear? Is that what you're so upset at being shut out from – the fact that your drunken old boyfriend is also an emotional cripple, a fucking mixed-up demented little fucking schoolboy?'

105

27

'It's all right, Dad,' says Michael. 'Don't try to speak. Please don't try to speak.'

With painful slowness Dennis lifts his hand to his face and drags the mask away from his mouth.

'Need to,' he whispers.

'Let it wait,' says Michael, 'until you've got more strength.'

Dennis closes his eyes momentarily, as if mustering his will. 'Honesty,' he says, before replacing the mask.

Michael sighs, a heavy sigh that seems to drain all his emotions away, that leaves him feeling hollow, numb. He doesn't want it to end like this. He draws in a deep breath, stands up, and walks across to the room's one window. He stares down at a small, grimy, concrete yard, packed with enormous green industrial waste bins. A hospital this size must produce an awful lot of waste of one kind or another, it's one of the largest hospitals in the country. He wonders what kind of waste is in those bins. It kills a few moments. He's got to pull himself together.

He swings round, forces his mouth into some sort of a smile, and returns to his father's side. He sits back down and hears himself – in a strange, breezy voice – say: 'You know, it was Gypsy who raised the alarm, came tearing around to my house, she did! Good old Gypsy, eh?'

Dennis just looks at him.

'Yes, good old Gypsy,' says Michael, his voice rising. 'What a dog, eh, Dad? Phil's taking care of her, by the way. She's fine. Don't you worry about your little dog, Dad, she's fine, she is.'

Dennis looks, and waits. Michael goes on.

'I thought to myself, she's damned clever to have found my house at all. It's not like she's been there very often, is it? You've not visited many times, Dad, have you really? Not many times.'

Dennis lifts his arm again, and Michael stops talking. The mask is removed, and Dennis says, quietly but clearly: 'Many times.'

Now it's Michael's turn to just look. He doesn't understand. Perhaps he misheard.

'Came,' says Dennis. 'Stood outside. Couldn't knock.'

'Oh, Dad,' says Michael, his normal voice returning. 'Oh, Dad.'

A spasm of pain shows itself in Dennis's face. The mask goes back on, and he appears to fall into a brief, tormented sleep. Michael struggles with himself, desperate to fight off the tears that are already beginning to sting his eyes. He knows, now, that it's up to him, that his father isn't about to give up, not until he has to – he's going to try and make his peace. He knows, too, that there isn't much time. Worst of all, he knows that Dennis won't be fooled by anything less than the truth. *But Jesus Christ,* he thinks. *Jesus Christ, why does it have to be now, like this, when it's too late to make amends? Why didn't he care what I was feeling when I needed him to, when Mum died? Why wouldn't he answer my questions? Why was he always so … so far away?*

Michael wants to scream. He wants to scream, and cry, and shout. He wants to hit someone, or break something. But more than that – more than anything – he wants his mum. He's thirty-eight years old and in pain and he wants his mum. But his mum is gone, and soon his father will be gone, too. Something inside him makes the decision. He'll give Dennis what he wants. He'll talk to him.

'Dad? Dad, are you awake?'

Dennis nods his head slightly, his eyes still closed.

'Dad, I know what you want. You want to put things right, before … '

Dennis slowly opens his eyes, and removes the mask once again. 'No,' he says.

'No?'

'No. Just want ... '

'What, Dad? What do you want?'

'Truth. Want to know ... problem.'

'You mean,' – Michael struggles to say it – 'between us?'

Dennis nods emphatically.

'Even though it's too late to change anything?'

For a few moments, Dennis says nothing, and Michael wonders if he's going to try and tell him that it's never too late. But he doesn't. He says, with a weary, profound sadness: 'Yes. Even if ... too late.'

As he speaks, the unit nurse passes by, glances over in their direction, and smiles at them both. 'Not too long without the oxygen,' she calls, brightly.

Michael watches her go, studies the clean, crisp lines of her uniformed shape as she makes her way across the room before disappearing through the double doors. He watches the doors as they swing back to their proper positions, as they flutter to a standstill. Then he turns back to his father, and he says: 'I don't know if I can do this. I find it so hard to talk about ... about the way I feel.'

A strange smile appears on Dennis's face. 'Chip off block,' he says.

'Perhaps,' says Michael, hurriedly, and the smile melts away.

Michael clears his throat, and trains his eyes on the cardiac monitor on the opposite side of the bed. 'When you came round to see me, last time,' he says, cautiously, 'you tried to talk to me about Mum.'

'Yes.'

'And I didn't want you to.'

'No.'

'Because I couldn't stand it. Because I'm all mixed up in my head about her, because you never let me talk about her after it happened. It was as if you thought I'd just forget about her if we didn't talk about her. But I needed to talk, Dad. I needed you to help me, and you didn't. You didn't help me.'

Dennis is silent, but for the rasping of his breath. The cardiac monitor beeps. The infusion pump whirs. 'Put your mask back on,' says Michael.

Dennis remains totally still, lost in a passing lifetime, until Michael moves to replace his mask for him and he shakes his head with a sudden furious energy. Michael retreats, startled. Dennis goes still again, staring up at the ceiling. Michael opens his mouth to speak, but his father beats him to it.

'Sorry,' he says.

A terrible silence follows while Michael searches inside himself for some kind of a response. He knows what his father wants to hear and he wants to say it, he truly wants to offer something forgiving. He wants to say that it doesn't matter. But he can't. Because it does matter. It'll always matter.

'Do you remember, Dad,' he says, slowly, 'when me and Phil went to stop with Aunt Eileen, when Mum was ready to have the baby? Do you remember that I didn't want to go, that I wanted to stay with her?'

Dennis shakes his head.

'You don't remember that I didn't want to go?'

'No.'

'Well, you see, that's something else that I've always ... blamed you for. I mean, I know that you couldn't have known what was going to happen. But I still felt that it was your fault. I felt that if you'd let me stay ... '

Dennis, still without the mask, opens his mouth. No words come out.

'I know, Dad,' says Michael. 'I know. It makes no sense. But you asked me to tell you what the problem is, and that's part of it. I think that's how it started. I felt I'd been pushed aside, shut out.

And I feel like you've shut me out ever since. I feel like I lost my entire family when Mum died, because it was Mum who bound us all together. It was Mum who noticed if we were feeling sad. It was Mum who made sure we knew we were loved. And when she went, there was just a man and two boys, living in the same house. But it needn't have been like that, Dad. If you'd have only let us talk about her, we could have kept her spirit there in the house with us, she'd have guided us. She dedicated her life to us, to you and me and Phil. We were all she had, and we were enough, I'm sure of it. But if she could have known what would happen to us after she'd gone, if she could see us now ...

'Look at us now, Dad. Look, I'm crying. You're crying. We're both crying and nothing's getting better, nothing's being solved. It's all just a huge bloody mess and nothing's being solved. Put your mask back on, Dad, for God's sake.'

28

'Mum, it's me again. I'm drunk again, ever so drunk. I've been trying not to, so much, drink, but a bad couple of days. Everything at once. Relentless. Dad, Clare, stupid stupid me, relentless.

'He's going to die, it won't be long. Have I told you? I must have told you. But when he goes, there'll be none of this. There'll be no talking to him like this.

'Am I bad? Am I bad because I can't say the things I don't mean? Why? It doesn't make everything all right, does it, that he's dying? It makes things worse. I was in the hospital, Mum, he couldn't breathe. He was gasping in front of me with no air and I was only telling the truth and Jesus Christ Almighty what am I?

'The truth, though, it's dangerous. I told Clare the truth. She was pushing me. She wanted to know what goes on in my head and I showed her. It just came pouring out. I shouldn't have let it happen like that. She was only trying to get close to me. And I've wanted to talk to her, but I just couldn't, Mum, just couldn't. She burst into tears, she went straight home. What's left, now, if she leaves me? What's left?

'A bad couple of days, Mum. Everything at once. Relentless.'

29

Formaldehyde is a dangerous substance. A taxidermist up in Scotland once blinded himself with it, carrying out the same procedure that Michael is involved with now.

He's injecting a solution of the chemical into a herring gull's foot, using a syringe given to him by a diabetic customer. The formaldehyde will fill out the bird's toes, and stop the fine leathery skin from shrinking down, wrinkled and dead, onto the bones. By the time the fluid dries out, it will have stiffened the skin, leaving it hollow, but correctly formed, and preserved from the inside. It's a technique that Michael came across in one of the trade journals, and it's worth the magazine's subscription all on its own.

He withdraws the needle from one fattened toe, and gently eases it into the next. The trick is to get the tip of the needle just beneath the surface of the skin, but above or beside the bone. Then it's a matter of squeezing very gently on the syringe. This, apparently, is where the Scottish taxidermist went wrong. He squeezed too hard, and the pressure forced the liquid back up out of the hole in a sudden jet that hit him straight in the eye. He wasn't even wearing safety goggles.

When he's finished the feet Michael ejects the remaining formaldehyde back into its bottle and stands back to assess his work. It's looking good – the gull's toes are nice and plump, and there's a faint but discernible sheen to the skin. The feet were the final stage of the bird's presentation, the finishing touch to a job well done. It's a straightforward mount, with the bird standing upright, wings folded, head slightly to the right. It looks just as it should. Another specimen finished.

He carries the bird into the showroom and places it on the shelf.

He strolls back into the studio and fetches a small block of polyurethane foam out of a cupboard. Over the next fifteen minutes or so, he will carve and sand and shape the block until it becomes the surrogate body of a large brown rat, ordered by a private collector in Essex.

If he was so inclined, Michael could spend half his life working with rats. The demand for them is high, not just from collectors, but from people who use them as props at pest control exhibitions, for health and hygiene training, during university lectures. And a lot of taxidermists refuse to handle them, which has always surprised him. Of all the animals, rats are amongst the most satisfying when it comes to creating the illusion of life. Their deeply gleaming eyes, their scaly, whipping tails, their snaggled yellow teeth and their incongruously dainty claws, all combine to convey a presence that death cannot annul.

Michael draws a rough body shape onto the side of the foam block and, steadying it on the bench, he cuts it out with a junior hacksaw. Once he has the basic form he begins the process of refining, rasping the material down and smoothing away the remaining edges until he's holding what looks like an oversized pumice stone.

He takes a rat skin from a wooden box beneath the window and gently stretches it around the shape. The body is too bulky generally, and particularly at the neck end. He makes a mental approximation of the measures required, removes the skin, and goes over to the cabinet to dig out some coarse sandpaper. He sands the shape briskly for a few moments, then retries the skin. After three repetitions of the process, the body is ready, and it's time for a cup of tea.

He's waiting for the kettle to boil when a hornet drones in through the open window, surveying the studio in a wide sweeping arc before settling on the worktop within inches of his resting hand. It's found an unwashed teaspoon encrusted with sugar, and Michael watches closely as it dedicates itself to the satiation of its craving.

It's now early September and in this latter part of their lives the workers are experiencing a new freedom. Their queen laid her final batch of eggs some time ago. Those eggs became larvae, and from those larvae came the male hornets which have already fertilised the new queens, helping to ensure another nest, in another place, in another year. There are no more little mouths to feed, and the workers' constant search for protein is over. Now they need act only for themselves. They are free to get what they want, and this one has found it.

The kettle starts to pop and sputter, vibrating the worktop to the extent that the teaspoon begins to rock on its back, but the hornet is unperturbed. It continues to feed, the minute machinery of its front legs and mouthparts a frenzied blur of gratification. Michael makes his tea. He pours the sugar straight from the bag, and stirs it with a pencil.

Sitting down with the drink, he reflects on the day's proceedings. The gull is finished, well on time, and he should manage to get the rat sewn up and mounted before he knocks off at about six. Then he'll go down to the chip shop for something to eat, before having a bath and catching the bus into Derby to meet Clare outside the cinema at eight.

It will be the first time he'll have seen her since the night of the storm, over a week ago. He's spoken to her on the phone, twice, and on both occasions there was a noticeable distance in her voice, an uncertainty. He doesn't blame her for that – he must have frightened her half to death with his ridiculous outburst. He frightened himself with it. He is just grateful, profoundly grateful, that she didn't finish with him there and then. Maybe she will, tonight. Maybe his apology, his deep sorrow, will not be enough. Or will she give him that second chance? Will they end the evening in her clean, warm bed?

His eyes are drawn upwards, up above the freezer. He gazes at the pike. 'What do you think, Mum?' he says. 'Have I managed to screw things up again?'

He walks over to the window and looks out. 'If Clare stays with me,' he says, 'I'm going to talk to her. I'm going to tell her all about myself, properly, and calmly. I'm going to make it right. And tomorrow night I'm going in to see Dad again, and ...

'And ...

'And, well, we'll see, won't we?'

30

Eileen is sitting by the side of Dennis's hospital bed. She is holding his hand. Dennis is propped upright with pillows, his sunken eyes peering dimly over the top of the oxygen mask. Beneath the mask, his open mouth has formed into a barely distinguishable smile. He is thinking about the time, some fifty-five years ago, when he shot his sister in the leg with a homemade bow and arrow.

It was a wonderful shot. She must have been thirty yards away, and running at a good pace. He hadn't actually expected to be able to hit a moving target from that distance. He hadn't expected his arrow, which was little more than a sharpened stick, to be so efficient, both in the air, and upon its meeting with Eileen's leg.

At the time, Eileen was not at all pleased, and Dennis himself had felt a sudden sickness of guilt in his stomach as she tumbled to the ground with a baffled cry. It was an unhappy incident. And yet, Dennis is glad that it happened. Because, as the years followed, and in the way of the best childhood pranks, it managed gradually to transform itself into something funny, something they could talk about, laugh about. It became one of the stories that connect Dennis to this prim, businesslike woman who is holding his hand. Dennis would like to retell the story now. He would like to remove the mask from his face and say, 'Eileen, do you remember when ...?'

But he no longer has the strength for such reminiscences. He is fading, and there will be no reprieve from this. There is a feeling in his chest that he has not felt before, a feeling of otherness. Despite the pain, which is constant, his lungs feel as if they are no longer a part of him, as if they have dissociated themselves, unprepared to share the dying with the man who spent a lifetime bringing about their ruin.

Dennis has his affairs in order. His will was sorted out many years ago. It's a simple document. His house will be sold and Michael and Phil will share the proceeds. His modest savings will go to the Anglican church on Wilne Lane.

Phil has been looking after Gypsy, and has agreed to give her a permanent home. It will do him good to have a dog. When he thinks of Gypsy, Dennis is grateful in his heart. He would like to see her, just once more, but he knows he will not. He knows his destiny is to die in this bed before morning.

He is not afraid of his destiny. He only wishes he had more time, time to make his peace with Michael. If he had only known the width of the valley that lay between them, he could have begun work on the bridge sooner, could have completed the job that he so clumsily began. Or not. Because, as he knows better than most, it is death's habit to arrive too soon. It came for his wife too soon, for their daughter, too soon. If Dennis has a dying wish, it is that death might be a little kinder to his sons.

'Dennis?' says Eileen.

He blinks an acknowledgement.

'It's nearly eight o'clock. I'm going to have to go in a moment. All right?'

He blinks.

'I'll see you again tomorrow. I'm coming in with Phil and Kate in the morning, and then Michael's coming in tomorrow night. OK?'

He blinks again, and this time there are tears.

Eileen stands up, still holding his hand. 'Now don't upset yourself,' she says. 'We'll all see you tomorrow.'

She stands awkwardly by the bed, her fingers entwined with his, waiting for him to signal that he is ready to let go. Dennis continues to hold on to her, watching her face, as his own glistens with increasing tears.

After the longest of minutes, she bends over and kisses him softly on the forehead. 'Good night, Dennis,' she says. 'You have a good sleep now.'

She gently prises his fingers away from hers with her free hand. She lays his arm down on the bed beside him. Then she turns around and walks swiftly out of the ward.

31

It's happening, but it's not happening to Michael. He is merely watching, as if he has found himself in someone else's dream. That cannot be right. It cannot be right that even at the funeral of his own father he is on the edge of the scene, observing.

In front of Michael is his father's plain coffin. Behind him is a small sea of dark suits. The church is practically full. Glancing over his shoulder, Michael sees several people that he recognises – local farmers, landlords, and the like. But many have faces he doesn't know. Who on earth are they? Where have they all come from?

Returning his gaze to the front of the church he notices the organist, getting ready to play the first hymn. He's tucked away behind two blue velvet curtains, but there's a gap between them which Michael can see through. The organist looks ancient. His eyes bulge. The flesh on his neck is creased and saggy, hanging in folds. He is almost entirely bald, but for the odd defiant strand of silver sprouting up and out from the crown of his mottled head. He's hunched forward over the keyboard, craning his neck to examine the sheet music as if he's reading it for the first time. It's *Abide With Me*. He must have played it a thousand times.

The minister utters a few words of introduction before announcing the hymn, and in the short silence between his voice ending and the music starting, a curious choking sound comes from somewhere over to Michael's right. It's Phil. He's crying. Kate has her left arm around his waist, and her right arm on his, as if helping him to stand. For the briefest of moments, and for the first time in his life, Michael feels a sorrow for his brother that isn't mingled with scorn. It's almost a good feeling. It's how a man should feel towards his grieving brother.

The music starts and the people sing and a huge wave of human sound rolls through the church. The people – all of the people – launch into the opening line with real feeling, real intent. There are many different kinds of voices; there are low voices, high voices, pure voices, gruff voices, and they're all bound together by the sound of the organ, each voice becoming part of something bigger than itself. Michael is taken aback by the sheer volume of it. The minister also seems pleasantly surprised and he fails, at first, to hide the fact.

The hymn ends, and the minister speaks.

'Dennis,' he says, 'was born in the tiny hamlet of Calke, where the Staunton Harold Reservoir now lies. Many of you here will no doubt remember Calke. You are able, perhaps, to close your eyes and see the valley as it used to be. It was, I hear, a place of great beauty, a tranquil place, and you may think it a pity that it had to change. But, on Earth, things do change. The seasons come and go. This is something we have to accept.'

Michael looks across at Phil again, but catches Eileen's eye instead. She gives him a tight, grim smile. He wonders if, like him, she is thinking of another, earlier funeral, with two coffins, one of them very small. A funeral at which Michael had done the crying, and Phil had been the quiet one.

The minister continues. 'At the age of twenty-two, Dennis had to move away from the family farm at Calke, to make way for the reservoir. Although very young, he took on a nearby farm, where he continued his trade of market gardening. It was not an easy trade, the industry was in a serious decline, but Dennis was a worker, and he had a passionate belief in the superiority of English-grown produce which drove him through the hard times.

'He had, it must be said, more than his fair share of hard times. His wife Nancy, mother to Michael and Phil, was taken into The Lord's care, along with their newborn daughter, many years ago.

120

It was a loss from which he never fully recovered, but he bore the burden of it himself. He was not a man to share his troubles.

'Nancy's death left Dennis with two young boys to raise, and it was no mean feat that he produced the two well-respected men that we have amongst us today. I am sure that he was very proud of both Phil and Michael, and they, too, should take pride in their father's memory.'

He looks deliberately at Phil, and then at Michael, and then back to his wider audience.

'It is never easy to sum up a life in a few short sentences. And it is no secret that I have to construct my image of Dennis's life largely through details given to me by his family and friends – I appreciate that most of you here will know more about Dennis than I do. However, I would like to add, if I may, my own impression of the man I saw, the man who was a regular member of this church's congregation for many years, long before I myself arrived in Woodington.

'When I did first arrive in this parish, of course, I had many people to meet. In order to effectively serve a community, a minister must try to get to know the members of that community, to form friendships, to forge trust. From the outset, I considered my duties in Woodington to extend beyond the walls of this building, but nevertheless, my priority was to attempt to form those friendships with the people who attend this church.'

He gives a wry smile. 'I am sure that Dennis would not mind me saying that he never intended me being his friend. He was always polite in his manner, but he never left me in any doubt that he did not come here to talk to me. He came here to talk to God.'

He smiles again, satisfied. 'And that is my simple contribution, my own personal image of Dennis: a quiet, decent, and private man, who found some solace in the company of Our Lord.'

The minister gazes mistily out across the heads of the people in his packed church, giving his words time to settle. Then he pads over to the lectern, opens his Bible, and says, 'Let us read now together, Psalm no 23: *The Lord is my Shepherd, I Shall Not Want.*'

32

It's quarter to ten on a Wednesday night, two weeks and one day since the funeral. Michael and Clare are sitting in The Prince of Wales, a small pub in the centre of Derby. Although it's midweek, the pub is alive with bustle and noise and hard-edged music. One of the two girls behind the bar has been helping herself to drinks ever since Michael and Clare arrived. From the state she's now in, it's apparent that she started well before that. The girl is laughing loudly, flirting outrageously with the male customers, and generally enjoying what will turn out to be the last night of her employment. The other girl mutters beneath her breath, casts dark looks in her direction, and tries to keep up with the serving.

Michael doesn't like it here, but he's determined not to let it show. He'll come into Derby and sit in a pub like this every night if that's what it takes to hold on to Clare. They've seen each other a few times now since his outburst, and have made love twice, but he knows that he hasn't been forgiven. He has tried his best to carry out his sincere resolution, has tried to open up his heart to her, but she's behaving as if she no longer cares. His pained and awkward attempts to speak of his father since the funeral have been tactfully brushed aside, worded away. He harbours the dread thought that, as with his father, it is already too late to make amends.

Perhaps, he tells himself, it's not as bad as he thinks. Perhaps she's just being unpredictable. Back in Woodington, in The Roebuck, he's forever overhearing men talk of the unpredictability of their women. Maybe she's being like those other women.

Except, he knows, she isn't like other women at all. She is an exquisite, intelligent, beautiful, fine person, more than any man could ever deserve. Definitely more than an evil little specimen like Andrew could ever deserve, a thought which still burns in his head, but which he will never again be foolish enough to give voice to. He has learned his lesson. Let it not be too late. *Please, please, please let it not be too late.*

Michael has a plan, a little idea that might just help things between them. 'I had a letter this morning,' he says.

'Oh, yes?' says Clare. 'What was that, then?'

'Have you ever been to Tenby?'

'I think so, once. It's in South Wales, isn't it?' She swirls the remaining half inch of her drink around in the bottom of her glass, and studies the effects.

'That's right,' says Michael. 'Well, they're closing down the natural history gallery in their museum, and they're going to sell off all the taxidermy. They want someone to give an independent valuation of their stock, and they've been given my name. It's just a matter of going down there for a day or so and seeing what they've got. Anything that's a bit tricky to put a price on I can research a bit when I get back, and then I'll send in a report later.'

'I see. And are you going to go?'

'I think so. It would be interesting, anyway – it's always good to see other people's work. It sounds as if they're prepared to pay me well, too.'

'You should do it, then,' she says.

He hesitates. 'Well, what I was thinking, actually, was that maybe you'd like to come down with me. I know it's not exactly the time of year for a holiday, but I thought I could get the valuations out of the way and then we could have two or three nights in a bed and breakfast or something.'

'Mmm, that sounds OK,' says Clare, but she still seems more interested in her glass. 'Does it matter exactly when you go?'

'Well, yes. They're shutting the museum down for a few weeks, for some rebuilding work, and they want me in on the first day, so they can get all the taxidermy put into temporary storage.'

'And what day is that?'

'The fourth of November, a Tuesday.'

'Oh, I'm sorry,' she says, her eyes finally meeting his. 'I won't be able to come.'

'Are you sure?' says Michael.

'I'm afraid so. But it was a nice gesture. Maybe we could –'

'Why can't you come?'

'I'll be away,' she says quickly. 'Now shall we have another drink, or shall we get off?'

'I don't mind,' says Michael.

'We'll have one more then, eh?'

She gets up and goes to the bar. The drunk barmaid is now giving free drinks to her customers too, but Clare stands away from the whooping gaggle that surrounds her, and is seen to by the other girl.

Once served, Clare remains at the bar for a short while, chatting with the other girl. Michael watches the back of her, watches her hair gently bobbing as she talks and nods. Her hand comes up to the side of her head, and she tugs lightly on her earlobe. Her fingers rest for a moment on her cheek, then she withdraws the hand as she throws her head back in laughter at something the girl has said to her. Michael wants to make her laugh like that, like she did on that first night in Woodington when they had tripped so lightly from pub to pub, when they had talked so easily about everything and nothing, when she had thrashed him mercilessly at pool and had feigned outrage upon hearing his favourite record on the jukebox.

Clare turns and comes back to their table, her smile fading with each step she takes. Michael can't bear to see the happiness go. Does she know how cruel she is being? Is it a considered act of punishment, this distancing, something she will stop doing when he has suffered sufficiently? Or is it the beginning of the end, already?

'I think,' says Clare, placing their drinks between them on the

125

table, 'that those two behind the bar are no longer the best of friends.'

Michael answers with a distracted nod. There's another question building in his mind, and he's trying to decide whether or not to air it. The question is, can Clare really not come away with him for a few days, or is it that she doesn't want to? Because the way she changed the subject so quickly, the way she was so keen to go and get another drink when lately she's been trying her best to slow him down, it's suspicious. Trying hard to maintain a casual tone in his voice, he asks her, 'What will you be doing?'

'Sorry?'

'You said you'd be away, on the fourth.'

Immediately, Clare begins to redden and Michael knows that something is amiss.

'Actually,' she says, 'I'm going to stay with my brother for a few weeks.'

'In Australia?'

'Yes. Perth.'

'Oh.'

She catches his eye, then looks away again. 'But it's not just that.'

'What do you mean?'

'I mean, it's not just a visit. There's something else.'

'Yes?'

'It's to help me make a decision.'

'About what?'

'I'm thinking,' she says slowly, 'of studying there for a while. There's a postgraduate teaching course they run at James's college.'

For a brief moment Michael doesn't fully understand what she is saying, and he's just about to respond when it sinks in.

'So,' she continues, 'this visit, in part, is to make sure it's definitely … what I want.'

Michael takes a deep breath. All of his worst fears are coming

126

true. She's not just going to finish with him, she's going to leave the country for good measure. He can barely bring himself to speak. 'But surely you can't ... Not just like ... '

'I was going to tell you,' she says. 'I wouldn't have just gone.'

'But what about us?'

She doesn't reply.

'And what about visas and permits and everything? It can't just be a matter of getting on a plane and signing up.'

'It's taken care of. I've made a provisional application and James says there's no reason why it shouldn't go through. If I like what I see I can go back to start in March. I can lodge with him and get some local work to fund myself.'

'And what about me?' asks Michael, his head in his hands now. 'Because I love you. I love you like I thought I would never love anybody. And I'll be over here.'

'I know,' says Clare, quietly. She pauses. 'Look, this Australia thing, it was something I was thinking about months ago, before we even met. I miss my brother and I want to spend some time with him. I'm sorry.'

'But I'm telling you that I love you!'

'Michael, how can you say that you love me? There's so much about me that you don't know, and you haven't exactly dealt well with the little you do. I'm not one of your creations, I'm not to be shaped by your hands.'

'For crying out loud,' says Michael, on the edge of tears, 'I don't want to control you. I just want to be with you, that's all. Don't you understand?'

'I don't know what I understand,' says Clare. 'I'm really, truly sorry, but there it is.'

33

Woodington's cemetery, which was once on the very outskirts of the town, is now surrounded on three sides by exclusive housing estates. If the land had been anything other than a consecrated site, it too would be supporting a collection of four-bedroomed homes by now. As things are, the cemetery serves to remind the town's newer arrivals that Woodington is not yet theirs. The dead at rest beside them, and the living that visit the dead, are the people Woodington belongs to.

Michael makes his way through the town, swapping the occasional nod with a fellow walker. He's going to the cemetery for what will be his second and, he suspects, his final visit. He just wants to confirm what he thinks he already knows – that he will stand by a rectangular patch of ground, with a piece of stone sticking up at one end, and will feel no different to the way he feels now.

There will be other visitors there, no doubt – it's a Sunday morning, with a clear sky and a warmth in the air that belies the fact that it's almost November. The other visitors will attend to their loved ones' resting places; they will replace dead flowers; they will draw some comfort from their efforts. But not Michael. For him, it will be like the funeral service all over again. He will be outside the ritual.

Michael approaches the open cemetery gates and gazes across the lines of graves, the stones lined up like mismatched dominoes. In the centre of the cemetery is a queer, spiky stone building. It's actually two buildings, two Chapels of Rest – one for the Church of England, one for the Nonconformists – connected and separated by a pointed gothic arch under which the finely gravelled footpath passes. Dennis's grave is at the far end of the cemetery, still out of sight.

There are, as Michael had expected, a number of people visiting their dead. Most of them are women, one of whom is using a pair of scissors to trim the grass around the bottom edges of a large granite cross. Another is gently rubbing at the top corner of a headstone with a wet cloth, removing some unwanted mark. They attend the graves; they draw comfort.

It is not until he passes through the Chapels of Rest archway that Michael sees his brother at their father's graveside. Phil is standing with his hands in his pockets. His shoulders are dropped and his head is hanging low. Gypsy sits forlornly at his side. Michael is strangely shocked at the sight. He can't make his mind up whether or not to approach them, but the decision is taken away from him when Gypsy turns and barks in half-hearted recognition.

Phil looks across at Michael, his face a confusion of despair and surprise. With visible effort, he draws his right hand from his pocket and raises it in welcome. For a split second, he looks like a younger version of Dennis. *Can't talk. Need to breathe.*

Michael goes over to join him, his boots scuffling through the piles of dead leaves that the previous night's wind has swept down to this end of the cemetery. 'Morning,' he says.

Phil doesn't reply. He just gives him a curious look that Michael can't decode. Embarrassed and bewildered, Michael redirects his attention to the patch of ground before them. He sees that the carnations at the base of the headstone are dying. Their pink and yellow heads are drooped, and streaks of brownish slime are beginning to form on their leaves. The wreath, too, is beginning to deteriorate, dark patches already appearing on the holly. Only the wreath's artificial berries are defying the decay around them, remaining bright and plastic, increasingly unreal. The grave itself, though, still looks as if it might have been filled yesterday, and the headstone, with its bright gold lettering carved deeply into the glossy black marble, will look new for a long time.

Michael looks across at Gypsy, who is still sitting in near total stillness and silence. He crouches down beside her, and strokes her face tenderly. 'Poor old thing, I wonder if she knows?' he says.

'Knows what?' says Phil.

'Where we are? I mean, I wonder if she knows that Dad's –'

'It's hard to tell,' says Phil abruptly. 'She's been like this ever since he first went into hospital.'

'Ah.'

'She's really missing him.'

'Yes.' Michael pauses, then he says, 'Well, I suppose when she's been with him all her life ... '

Phil gives him a strange, accusing look. 'Meaning?'

Michael stands back up and faces him. 'Nothing,' he says. 'I was just saying.'

'Just saying what?'

Michael averts his eyes. This has started badly, and it's quickly getting worse.

'Don't you miss him?' says Phil.

'Look,' says Michael, 'I –'

'You don't, do you?' He's almost shouting.

'Phil, I –'

Phil turns to leave. 'Come on, Gypsy. Let's go.' He tugs on her lead but she resists, her small frame rigid with indignation.

Michael reaches out and grabs the sleeve of Phil's jacket.

'Michael, what are you doing!' says Phil. 'Let go of me!'

'No,' says Michael.

Phil's eyes are dark with fury and grief. 'Let go,' he hisses.

'No. I want us to talk. Now. Don't you see, we're all that's left.'

He lets go of Phil's arm. 'There, I've said it. It wasn't quite how I wanted to say it, but ... What I mean is I want us to try and be brothers. I want us to be able to talk to each other. I'm sick of not being able to talk. I'm sick of it, it's no good. If we can't get on

– I mean, genuinely get on – then that's the family gone. Mum's family.'

Phil glares at him, his anger barely in check.

Michael winces, realising what he's done. 'And Dad's,' he says, quietly, waiting for the rebuke.

It doesn't come. Phil's face suddenly softens, and he says, 'Mum's been dead a long time, Michael.'

'And Dad's been dead for over a month,' says Michael.

'Yes.'

'And our sister never had a chance to live.'

'No.'

'So, however you look at it, that just leaves us.'

'Yes,' says Phil. 'I suppose it does.'

They immediately lapse into one of their familiar silences, but Michael is determined not to let it happen. 'Shall we go now?' he says, hurriedly. 'We could take a walk back to my house, have a coffee or something?'

Phil thinks it over for a moment. 'All right.'

'Come on, then,' says Michael, and they begin to make their way back through the cemetery, Gypsy making several attempts at staying before accepting the inevitable and falling into a steady trot at Phil's side.

'Kate and the kids at home, are they?' asks Michael, determined to keep the conversation alive, even at the cost of a little small talk.

'Yes,' says Phil. 'I wanted to come alone. It's … ' His voice trails off, as if he's thinking of something else, and all of a sudden he says: 'He did love us, you know, Michael. Both of us.'

Michael doesn't answer.

'He loved us,' says Phil.

Michael tries to keep his voice steady, tries to fight the resentment that still sits inside him like a stone. 'How do you know?' he says, carefully.

'I just do,' says Phil. 'He couldn't bring himself to show it, that's all. He wasn't that kind of man.'

'He always managed to show plenty of affection to his dogs.'

'And they showed it back, Michael, didn't they? They didn't try to understand him. They didn't sit around agonising about their relationship with him. They were loved, and they loved in return. They had faith. Take poor old Gypsy here, did she ever ask for proof?'

'And if it was good enough for his dogs, it should have been good enough for us, is that what you're saying?'

'It was enough for me, Michael. It was always quite obvious to me that he loved us.'

'I see,' says Michael. 'So I should have found it obvious, too?'

'Yes, you should.'

'Well, I didn't. I didn't find it obvious, not at all. Because it's not enough, Phil. It's not enough to drop a few invisible clues and expect other people to find them. I didn't even know Dad. I didn't know anything about him. I never felt like I was part of his life.'

'Well that's you, Michael. And you're not like everyone else, as you're always so keen to prove, with your oh-so-quirky pet bloody hornets and your precious pissing animals that you go on about like you're the only person in the world who's ever stuffed one ... '

Michael stops in his tracks, Phil's words hitting him like a slap in the face.

Phil stops too. 'I'm sorry,' he says. 'I didn't mean that. I don't know where it came from.'

Michael looks into his brother's embarrassed face, as if he's seeing him for the first time. 'It's all right,' he says.

'Really, I –'

'It's all right.'

They walk on in painful silence, past the supermarket, past the newly opened fitness club, and on to Michael's house.

132

34

It's the second day of November, a cold day. A hornet moves slowly over the slabs in Michael's back yard. Its body is a burden, a weight it can hardly carry. It drags the mass of itself in wide, futile circles.

What is it doing? Is it trying to go home, one last time? Someone should tell it, that can't happen. Because your home is up there and you are down here. You are down here on the cold ground, and life is beginning to leave you.

Be assured, hornet, you have struggled well; you are the very last. Your fellow servants have perished. Your queen, the mother of you all, died weeks ago, and the new queens have long since departed. They are tucked away in the nooks and the crannies, they have a winter to survive.

There will be no winter for you. You were born to work, and your work is done.

Hornet, you are crawling towards the end. Do you suffer? Do you understand the battle being fought within you? Do you feel your will diminish beneath the weight of the slowing?

Perhaps not.

Perhaps the will does not diminish. Perhaps it continues regardless, even as the body falters. You push forward, while you can. You do, while you can. Because to do, that is your mantra, and no one has told you how to stop.

You drag your body across the slabs.

A blackbird lands nearby. Vaguely, you sense its presence, but you cannot flee. You keep on moving, with an aching slowness. The blackbird scans the yard, until his glistening eye finds you. He dances towards you, he skips around you. He tips his sheeny head to one side, the better to come to a decision.

You drag your body across the slabs.

The blackbird's face appears before you. It is a dark, featureless mass. You are practically blind now, your senses are no longer reporting back.

The blackbird decides no and takes to the sky. You are swayed by the rush of air from his wings. You don't feel it. You drag your body. You fight against the slowing.

You are no longer aware of the ground that scrapes beneath you. You are no longer aware of anything. When you fall into a gap between the slabs, nothing has changed. You push forward.

The gap narrows; it tightens around your body. Everything is closing. Nothing has changed. You push.

You reach the end. There is nowhere left to go. You push. You do while you can. This is your meaning.

Death is coming.

Death is coming, and you will push your meaning beyond it.

35

Clare wakes to a new Perth morning. She arrived late the previous night, and after an over-tired, over-emotional reunion with her brother went straight to bed. Her sleepy eyes now open to reveal a room that she scarcely noticed when she first entered it.

It's a clean, unfussy bedroom, painted a simple light blue, with dark stained floorboards. James has obviously rearranged its contents for her benefit, and has pushed suitcases and boxes of books to the end of the room, where they sit beneath the window. The sun shines through strongly when she raises the blinds. She can hear James moving around in the kitchen, where he is preparing breakfast, preparing to look after her. Her big brother. James.

He is whistling softly to himself when she enters the kitchen, a song she recognises but can't name. He has his back to her and for a moment doesn't know she is there. Then he turns and sees her, and breaks into his trademark grin. 'Are we back from the dead, then?'

'I was so dreadfully tired last night,' she says. 'I got next to no sleep on the plane. I wanted to talk, but I barely had the strength to stand.' She is so happy she has to fight the tears.

He comes towards her. 'Don't you worry,' he says, 'we've got plenty of time to talk now.' He circles his arms around her and hugs her tight. 'God, it's good to see you, Sis.' They both smile, James at his unintentional poetics, and Clare because no one else in the world can call her 'Sis' and she's missed the sound of the word.

They talk animatedly through breakfast, Clare updating him with family news, and James telling her of his working life at the college, of the nightlife in the city, of his love life which is sporadic and, he insists, wholly satisfactory. Clare beams as she listens to him. He's the same James.

Once the pots are cleared, he says, 'How about we go for a drive? I've just bought myself a rather nice convertible Toyota.'

'That would be lovely,' she says. 'Show me Australia!'

An hour later James parks the Toyota at a pull-in on the edge of Kings Park. They are overlooking the Swan River, its broad banks looping away into the distance. He points out Narrows Bridge, which sweeps across the river in a clean brushstroke of bullet grey, its supporting pillars snug in the water. Cars cross it at intervals, with the alluring calm of distance.

Beyond the bridge are the beginnings of the city proper, a number of gleaming high rise blocks rooted amongst the riverside trees. 'I stop here sometimes on the way home from work,' he continues, 'and just read for a while, or just sit and look.'

'It's quite a view,' says Clare, sitting and looking.

'If you fancy a bit of a walk, I'll point out the Swan Bells.'

'Sounds good to me.'

They get out of the car and he leads her along a track which picks its way through the palms and tufty undergrowth. Clare can feel the heat of the midday sun radiating through her, warming her bones. Lizards start at their footsteps and dash into the brush to clear the way. The air is clear and the breeze is sweet.

After twenty minutes the track returns to the edge of the park, and another view of the city is before them. With the bridge no longer in evidence, and a hundred newly revealed tower blocks jostling for attention, the city seems to Clare to be suddenly less exotic.

'You should see it at night,' says James, as if he knows what she is thinking. 'When the neon's lit and it's all in silhouette, it's something else.'

Clare raises her hands in front of her face and makes a frame with her fingers, as if composing a photograph. 'So where are these bells?'

He reaches for her wrist and pulls her arms gently to the side, the camera of her fingers panning along the far bank of the river. 'You see the really wide tower block? The stubby one?'

'Yes.'

'Well just to the right of that, there's a tall glass tower.'

'Yes, I've got it!'

'And at the base of the tower is the bell chamber.'

'Oh yes. Isn't it strange?'

'The bells themselves were from England, a gift to Australia back in the Eighties. They're almost three hundred years old.'

Clare lets her hands fall and concentrates her gaze on the incongruous structure. Copper orange, and swollen like a ship's sail, the bottom half sits squat beside the river, whilst its slender tower emerges from its heart to rise high above it like an enormous mast.

'I think it's rather beautiful,' she says. 'Can we go for a closer look?'

'Of course,' says James. 'And there's a really nice little gallery nearby. We can pay a visit there to finish off the trip.'

'Sounds perfect.'

He gestures back towards the path. 'Let's go, then.'

By the time they're in the city, seeking out the bells, Clare's body has begun to feel heavy, the jetlag catching up with her. She is taken, though, with the cleanliness and order of Perth, the assured ambition of its architecture, its convincing mix of the old and the new. The Swan Bells themselves, up close, are also an impressive combination of past and future. Ringed by reflective pools of water, the glass and copper housing is decidedly modern, but the nautical styling and centuries-old cargo speaks of timeless tradition. She imagines the sound of the bells, singing across the city, bells made in England all those years ago bringing their songs to this place of energy and light.

The gallery, too, is delightful, specialising in contemporary Aboriginal art. Without exception the paintings are celebratory, uplifting, vibrant. There are swirling spirit landscapes of russet and gold, bright mandala-style flowers orbiting their ancient secrets, lucid ladders of colour glowing richly on the canvas. They are ordered yet fluid, dreamlike yet earthy.

The gallery owner appears and guides Clare to one end of the room, explaining, 'Aborigines use art and song to document and remember. Their paintings are stories. Stories of the land.' He indicates a particular picture. 'What do you see?'

Clare smiles. She doesn't doubt the man's sincerity, nor his desire for a sale. The painting is acrylic on canvas, and consists of a background of fine horizontal lines varying from light grey to black, via a dozen shades of mud and clay. Superimposed are three snaking trails of white, with footprints also in white and pawprints in brown, tracking across the scene. 'I don't know exactly what it represents,' says Clare, 'but it obviously suggests a journey.'

'That's right,' says the man. 'This painting is called *Possum Ancestor*. It tells of the ancestors who travelled to hunt the Possum. The undulating lines are the trail of the Possum, who was said to move both above and beneath the earth.'

'I see.'

'It's not abstract, this painting. It's real, specific.'

'How do you mean?'

'It's set in an actual place, a couple of hundred kilometres or so north-west of Alice Springs. It's a page from a history book, a page from a family album. It's about a real journey in more than one sense. The Aborigines, my artists, know that life itself is a journey.'

Clare smiles again, a little more cynically. 'Your artists?'

The man smiles back, caught out but not embarrassed. 'I don't mean my artists. I mean the artists I represent. It's just I'm very proud to deal in their work. I get quite paternal.'

'I understand,' says Clare. 'These paintings are very beautiful.'

'Indeed they are. It's the economy, that's what I love. The simplicity of form.'

'Yes,' says Clare, frowning, 'I'm an artist myself, and I'm beginning to think I've overlooked simplicity. I've become too involved with big ideas that I don't really own.' She glances across at James who is loitering by the door, obviously keen to be moving on, but in her mind she sees a sketch of a crow, hanging on the wall of her room in England. She knows, without doubt, that it's the best thing she's ever produced. The gallery owner is looking at her, eagerly. 'So, how much?' she says. 'I've got to warn you, I'm not rich.'

36

High in the early evening sky, high above the Staunton Harold
Reservoir, millions of particles of carbon swirl and blow in the air.
Tiny droplets of water, and a thousand different gases, swim amongst
and around these particles. It is smoke, but smoke so diffused that
it appears not to be there. It is a substance changed, a solid thing
transformed. It has become an irretrievable, unquantifiable, and
everlasting component of the universe.

Follow an imaginary line, as the crow might fly, from the Staunton
Harold Reservoir to Woodington, and the density of the particles
gradually increases, until the smoke becomes something tangible,
something visible. Above the red-tiled roof of The Woodington
Arms it is a widely cast veil, its pale fabric shredded by the wind.

The residents of Packhorse Road, should they happen to look
out of their terraced cottage windows, will see it darkened, a
burgeoning grey mass that moves more heavily, that lumbers and
folds and struggles in the sky.

At its source near the centre of the town it is a seething, boiling
blackness, an angry billowing cloud.

Michael's studio is on fire.

The fire started at the showroom end of the studio, and all of the finished specimens have succumbed to it. The flames have torn across the wooden flooring, into the workshop side, and the legs of Michael's workbench are now well alight. A bookcase has keeled over and some of the books have been propelled across the room. A copy of C.R. Hoben's *Practical Taxidermy* lies open near the sink unit, its pages rapidly becoming ash. Posters peel off the walls and are gone before they touch the floor. A cupboard door drops from its hinges, revealing a number of plastic containers that melt away in an instant, their contents exploding in a violent burst of white heat.

The blackened glass on the front of the pike's cabinet shatters, and the wooden framework begins to buckle and twist. The pike's pelvic fins curl up tight beneath its body, which erupts with crackling blisters all along its length. Its painted shell contracts, and the head tilts backwards, and the jaws open wide. The small blue button shimmers and softens and falls away from its face, into the flames. A moment later the pike is gone.

His head aches, spots of rain are beginning to appear on the windscreen of the van, and it's a long way home from Tenby, but Michael has a wry smile on his face. It was almost cruel what he did yesterday to the woman at the museum, but he was, after all, only defending his craft.

The woman, the museum's new curator, had made no attempt to disguise her delight at seeing the natural history gallery being closed down. 'People don't want it any more,' she said, in a decidedly accusatory tone. 'It's like zoos, isn't it? People don't want them. They want to see animals in their natural environment. And I have to say, I think that's right.'

Michael didn't answer her. He decided instead to set to work immediately, examining the exhibits and making notes.

Many of the exhibits were, in fact, far removed from any kind of convincing environment. The groundwork in some of the cases was decidedly amateur, and many of the creatures themselves were presented in outrageous poses. The worst example of all was a Victorian presentation of hummingbirds. Seven of these exquisite creatures were crammed together in a tall glass dome, their expressionless bodies almost touching, their feet wired onto the straggling branches of some wholly theoretical tree. Seeing this display of ineptitude, with these truly beautiful birds robbed of their natural grace, bothered Michael deeply. What made it worse was the practical certainty that they had been killed specifically for the purpose of featuring in this tawdry display. Looking at it, Michael could almost understand how the curator had come by her objections. Ironically, he also knew that this abomination – this undeniable evidence of the chequered history of his craft – would be quick to sell, albeit at a modest price. With a sigh, he made an entry in his notebook to this effect.

Not all of the exhibits, however, were so depressing. There were some genuinely awe-inspiring pieces amongst them, most notably a magnificent golden eagle, mounted with enormous skill and understanding. It was a huge specimen, well over two feet tall, and perfect in every detail, from its thick, densely-muscled legs to its fiercely hooked raptor's beak. Perched on a simple tree stump, the eagle was hunched forward, its mighty bronzed wings beginning to spread, as if ready to launch itself at a split second's notice. Its searing hunter's gaze and the sheer authority of its bodily presence made it impossible to ignore.

Michael spent what remained of the morning carefully inspecting and cataloguing the contents of the gallery. The curator woman didn't seem to have a lot to do, but still managed to keep herself so busy in the background that she didn't find the time to offer him a drink. At lunchtime he took himself to a nearby pub where he ate his meal quietly and alone, and booked himself a room for the night.

After lunch he returned, and spent a little while looking around the rest of the museum before getting back to the taxidermy. The museum was relatively small, but quite ambitious, with a particularly impressive archaeology section. It had an art gallery displaying the paintings of a local artist who was quite obviously, and justifiably, a source of great pride in the town. One of his exhibits, a shadowy portrayal of two craggy old sailors playing dominoes at a pub table, was as poignant and evocative a painting as Michael had ever seen.

To its credit, the museum seemed keen to attract children. There were numerous activity sheets dotted around the place, encouraging them to engage with the various items on display. Michael noticed, too, a proliferation of children's response slips, questionnaires asking for their opinions on what they had seen.

He finished his assessment at half past five in the afternoon. The curator had still managed not to speak to him, apart from giving civil answers to the occasional necessary question. By this time, Michael had decided that it was not merely a distaste for taxidermy that was behind her distinctly unfriendly disposition. Perhaps he reminded her of someone who had done her a great injustice. Maybe she didn't like anyone. Either way, he had decided not to let her off too lightly. He weighed up the odds, and took a chance.

'That's me done,' he said, cheerily. 'I'll get the details written up and sent in over the next few days for you.'

'Thank you,' she said.

'Right, I'll be off, then.' He made as if to leave, taking a few steps, before spinning back round.

'Oh,' he said, 'I nearly forgot. There's one more thing I meant to ask.'

'Yes?'

'Those bits of paper you've got, for the kids. Wanting to know what things most interest them?'

He saw her flinch, visibly. 'Yes?'

'One of the questions ... '

'Yes.'

'Of all the things you've seen on your visit today, what was your favourite?'

'What about it?'

'I just wondered what most of them thought.'

'You know what children are like,' said the woman. 'A lot of them just use it as an excuse to write something stupid. There isn't the discipline these days.'

'But most of them give a straight answer?'

She couldn't avoid it. He wasn't going to let her. 'Yes.'

'What is it?' asked Michael.

If looks could kill, he would have died a thousand times.

'The golden eagle,' she said, stiffly.

39

It's ten minutes to midday when Michael arrives back home. Thirty minutes later his van comes screeching to a halt outside the newsagent's shop near Clare and Jaz's house. He jumps out of the van, slams the door shut behind him, and strides down the narrow alley to the immediate right of the shop. At the end of the alley he finds a tiny courtyard, with a flight of metal steps zigzagging up to a grimy blue door on the first storey. He climbs the steps, and starts to bang his fist on the door.

Bang bang bang. His violent hammering echoes all around him, the sound trapped between the tightly packed buildings. Bang bang bang. *Open this door or I will kick it down.*

The door opens, Andrew is standing there. Maybe he has that familiar sneer on his face. Maybe he looks suddenly afraid. Michael is oblivious; he sees without seeing. He lunges forward, raising both of his hands to Andrew's throat as if to strangle, then at the last moment he twists his palms outwards and shoves them hard into his face, pushing him back into the building. Andrew stumbles, loses his balance, and goes crashing backwards onto the worn red carpet of the hallway. He scrambles to his feet but Michael is there to meet him, with a swinging right-hander that catches him on the nose and snaps his head sideways. Again he stumbles, this time keeling through an open doorway at the bottom of the hall. Michael follows him in.

Andrew is standing tight against the chimney breast, flattened against it, as if trying to merge into it. His nose is pouring with blood. 'For fuck's sake,' he says, trembling, wide-eyed. 'What are you doing? What are you fucking doing?'

'I'm going to kill you,' says Michael, and he steps forward.

40

After, Michael drives straight from Andrew's flat to Phil and Kate's house. He drives slowly, mechanically. As he turns into their estate, he begins to sing to himself in a queer, spiky voice that is not his own: '*And they all get put in boxes, little boxes, all the same.*' It's a line from a song that came out in the Sixties. It became a minor classic, and it still gets played. There's another line in that song, something about the houses being made of 'ticky-tacky.' Michael used to like that line. Some less than kind part of him had sympathy with its sentiments, the way it looks down on people whose lives are flat and ordinary, people who don't manage to escape into other worlds through art or alcohol, or whatever it might take. People who live on nice estates like this, with their neat and useless bits of front lawn, their brick-paved drives on which they stand on a Sunday morning, to exchange pleasantries with the neighbours as they wash their sensible cars. Michael used to view such people as insignificant, and the song helped justify it. But he was wrong. Because good people live on estates like this. Kate lives here, and she's his friend.

He arrives at the house and knocks on the door. A little of Andrew's drying blood smears itself onto the white woodwork. He pulls his sleeve over his fist and rubs at the stain until it disappears.

The door opens. Phil is standing there.

'Michael,' he says, 'you're back.'

'I want to see Kate,' says Michael.

'Michael, you're covered in blood! What on earth's happened?'

'I want to see Kate.'

'Yes. Look, have you been home yet?'

'I want to talk to Kate,' says Michael. 'She's my friend.'

'Yes,' says Phil, awkwardly. 'Well, you'd better come in.'

He lets Michael through. As he enters, Emily and Nathan appear at the foot of the stairs.

'Everything all right, Uncle Michael?' asks Emily.

'No,' says Michael, his voice hollow.

'Everything all right, Dad?' asks Nathan.

'I don't know. Just go back to whatever you were doing, will you?'

Nathan looks at his sister. She shrugs. They don't move. Kate descends the stairs behind them. 'Do what your father asks,' she says. 'Now, please.'

She stands aside to let them pass, and the two of them make their way up, whispering to each other as they go.

'What's going on?' says Phil.

'I've told you,' says Michael. 'I've come to talk to Kate.'

Phil turns towards her, his face a question.

'It's all right,' says Kate. 'If Michael wants a little chat, that's fine.'

Phil clears his throat. 'Shall I get us all something to drink, then?'

'Good idea,' says Kate. 'Sweet tea for Michael, I think. Then perhaps you could leave us alone for a while, if you don't mind.'

Phil sounds every bit as confused as he looks. 'Yes,' he says. 'That is, no. Of course I don't mind. I'll, er, make some ... ' He goes off into the kitchen.

'Right,' says Kate, pointing towards the door on Michael's left. 'Use the sink in there. Get yourself cleaned up, and I'll meet you in the lounge.'

'I think I might have killed someone,' says Michael. 'I hit him and he fell and his head hit the hearth and he went all still and there was blood everywhere and –'

'Forget the cleaning up,' she says. 'Come on through.'

'So,' she says, when they are in the lounge. 'You know about the fire at your studio? You've been home?'

'Yes, it was this bloke called Andrew he did it so I went round to where he lives and he was there and I –'

'Wait, Michael. Just slow down. You know who started the fire?'

'Yes.'

'And the person who did it, that's the man you hit?'

'Yes. But I didn't mean –'

'Michael, wait. Let me help you.'

'Yes. I'm sorry.'

'Where is this man now?'

'Where I left him. At his flat.'

'Which is where, exactly?'

'Marcus Street, Derby. Above the newsagent's.'

Kate reaches over from her seat and picks up the telephone. 'I'm going to phone for an ambulance,' she says.

Michael shudders. 'All right.'

'I'm also going to ask for the police. I'm going to tell them that you're here, and that they can come and collect you. You agree that it's the right thing to do? For this man you hit, and for yourself?'

'Yes. Yes, I suppose it is.'

'Then once all the facts are established, and this thing settles down as it will, I promise I'll help you in any way I can. OK?'

'Yes,' says Michael. 'Yes, I know you will.'

'Good,' says Kate, and she makes the call, before going to see what's taking Phil so long with the tea.

41

Yagan, an Aborigine tribal leader killed in the early 1800s, is now remembered in bronze on Heirisson Island, in the middle of the Swan River. Originally friendly with the first European settlers, Yagan was nonetheless compelled by Aboriginal law to avenge the killing of a young member of his clan who had been shot for entering a settler's homestead. Yagan and his comrades went to the ranch and speared a man to death. These events began the story that would lead to Yagan's downfall, and his preserved head being sent to England, where it was exhibited in the Liverpool City Museum until 1964. His statue depicts a lean but densely muscled man, a sculpture on either side of death. He is naked, with his barbed spear borne horizontally across his shoulders. He stares forever towards the city, unconquered and unbowed.

James and Clare are sitting on a bench near the statue. They too stare out towards the shimmering city. They have cycled over the causeway which connects the island to Perth, James on his mountain bike, and Clare on an old-fashioned racer borrowed from a neighbour. The bikes now lay at their feet, sprawled upon the ground like exhausted lovers.

A large male grey kangaroo hops nonchalantly into the scene, in a casual search for sweeter grasses. It turns towards them, silhouettes itself briefly against the glassy water, twitches its sooty nose and bounds away. It leaves a greater silence than it entered.

'So what will you do?' says James, eventually.

'I don't know.'

The silence hovers.

'Do you want to phone Mum and Dad?'

'No.'

Another kangaroo appears, a hesitant young joey not yet steady on its feet. Its eyes widen at the sight of the two humans, and its pointed ears stiffen with fright. An urgent clicking sound erupts from its throat.

'It's lost its mother,' says James.

Before Clare has time to respond, the mother appears, answering her offspring with a deeper clucking of her own. Within a moment, the two have bounded off into the undergrowth.

The silence is worse than ever.

James clears his throat. 'So how –'

'I don't know.'

'Will –'

'James, please!'

The day is beginning to fade. Yagan's shadow is darkening on the scorched earth, and the city lights are beginning to come on across the water, one by one.

'Everything seems suddenly unreal,' says Clare.

James glances at her, but says nothing, waiting for her to continue.

'I feel like I don't know who I am.'

'You're you!' says James, emphatically.

'Yes, and suddenly I don't know what that means.'

'It'll be all right. It's a shock, that's all.'

Clare flicks out her foot and nudges the front tyre of the borrowed racer, which spins for half a revolution before coming again to a halt. She thinks of the bright mandala patterns of Aboriginal art in the gallery near the Swan Bells, of the very essence of life they somehow embodied.

'You know,' she says quietly, 'I've been studying art, one way or another, for years. And I'm no great artist, and I'm no great scholar. I never will be.'

'What are you talking about?' says James. 'You've done some

lovely stuff.'

'Not really. A few nice sketches maybe.'

'Clare, this isn't you. You're starting to worry me.'

She reaches over and squeezes his hand tightly. 'Don't be silly. Just listen, will you?'

'It depends what you've got to say.'

She gives the tiniest of smiles. 'You were always my protector, weren't you? When we were little, I used to really believe there was nothing you couldn't do. I always thought, as long as you were around, everything would always be all right. I've never lost that.'

'I know.'

'When you came over here, it almost broke my heart. Isn't that stupid?'

James speaks quietly. 'It's not stupid, Sis, but ... '

'What?'

'Nothing.'

'No, tell me.'

He hesitates. 'Well, I wasn't always comfortable, being the hero, let's just say that.'

She stares at him in surprise. 'Pardon?'

He averts his eyes. 'That belief you had in me. I almost felt it was, I don't know, some kind of avoidance thing.'

'Avoidance of what?'

'I'm not sure. Living your own life? Having to find your own strength? Something like that.'

She continues to stare at the side of his face. 'James, I don't believe this! Here I am, my world suddenly turned upside-down, and you're telling me I've been a liability all my life.'

'Oh, come on, I never said that.'

She stands up and takes several strides towards the water, before spinning around, her face full of pain. 'What's going on here, James? You've never talked like this before.'

'Clare, calm down. You're blowing everything out of

proportion.'

'Oh, it's Clare now, is it?'

'Clare ... Sis ... Jesus! What's the matter?'

'Is that why you came here?'

'What?'

'Is that why you disappeared to the other side of the world, to get away from your clinging little sister?'

'Of course not. I came for lots of reasons.'

'And I was just one?'

'No! I wanted a new life that's all. A life of my own. Sometimes you have to strike out, take a risk, follow your instincts.'

She takes her eyes off him and looks again towards the city. 'Are you referring to me now?'

'No, I'm not. I wouldn't presume, I'm not the right person. Talk to Jaz. Talk to Mum, even. But whatever you do, just make sure it's your decision. Look to yourself, that's all.' His tone is almost imploring. 'Just, look to yourself.'

42

Michael stands outside his back door, staring down through the darkness at the bleak silhouette of his burnt-out studio. He knows that sooner or later he will have to go and take a closer look, but he can't do it now. He can't face it. He's only been in a police cell for a few hours, but it's left him feeling dirty, corrupted, worthless.

Certainly, he is now a criminal; he has a criminal record. The patterns on the ends of his fingers have been mirrored and filed away. A document exists, giving details of his height, the colour of his hair, the colour of his eyes. A swab was taken of the inside of his cheek, so that the code of his DNA could be determined and retained. It's a routine procedure, carried out after all arrests; the resulting database of samples is of use in the capture and conviction of re-offenders, and the as-yet uncaught. It's often how rapists and murderers are brought to book. Michael wonders if the powers that be think he might commit rape or murder one day. Maybe they suspect he already has, and that subsequent cross-referencing will bring the crime to its solution.

Not that the police officers themselves seemed to think that of him. They were surprisingly kind. The grey-haired officer who had arrested him, and who had carried out most of the associated enquiries, seemed keen to spare him any unnecessary discomfort. In fact, it was more than that, he was decidedly friendly. A soft touch, maybe. Perhaps that's how he reached middle age without being promoted from the rank of constable. Whatever, Michael was grateful to him.

The officer had escorted Michael to the police station, uncuffed, and stayed with him in the custody suite while the custody sergeant went through the necessary procedures. Michael was frisked, and a metal detector was passed around his body. He was asked to produce his wallet, which was gone through, then he had to empty the contents of his pockets. The custody sergeant was visibly amused when it came to the three glass eyes, less so when it came to the penknife. The various articles were documented, then placed in a large plastic bag which was sealed and tagged in front of him, before he was taken to his cell.

'I'm going to have to ask you to remove your belt, Mr Marshall,' said the officer, at the cell door.

'My belt?'

'Yes, please. It's routine.'

Michael's puzzlement must have shown, because the officer soon continued: 'We have to take all reasonable precautions to prevent attempts at suicide.'

'Oh, I see,' said Michael.

'And you can either take your boots off and leave them outside, or if you really want to keep them on, you can remove the laces.' He smiled, encouragingly. 'Most people just take them off altogether.'

'Yes,' said Michael, 'I'll, er ... ' He bent over and took off his boots. The tiled floor was cold beneath his feet.

The officer led him into the cell.

'You'll remain here while I go and get a statement from the man you assaulted, and assess the extent of his injuries. Would you like a blanket?'

'No, thank you.'

'Well, if you change your mind, or if you want something else, you just push this button here, and someone will come. OK?'

Michael glanced at the small red button. Apart from the thin blue mat on the bunk, it was the only item of colour in the cell.

'Yes. Thank you.'

The officer smiled again, at the door. 'Right you are, then,' he said. 'I'll see you later.'

'Thank you,' said Michael, and the door closed heavily, and he shivered.

It was two hours later when the officer returned and took Michael back into the interview room.

'Now, then,' he said, across the table, 'I've been to see the man you assaulted. He has a broken nose, a dislocated jaw, a cut to the forehead, and mild concussion. He also has one hell of an attitude towards the police, and a deep dislike of you. He's hoping that you're going to get sent to prison for this, but I think that's very unlikely. We're going to charge you with "actual bodily harm". You'll be bailed shortly, to appear in front of the next available magistrate's court. That should be within the next two or three days. You've admitted the offence, you have no previous convictions as far as we know, and something tells me you're not a natural born killer, so my guess is you'll be looking at community service. How does that sound?'

Michael sighed. 'It sounds like something that happens to criminals.'

The officer looked briefly displeased. 'Now then, you're not about to say it wasn't you after all, are you?'

'No,' said Michael, sadly. 'It was definitely me. It just doesn't feel like it was. I can hardly even remember doing it. Something just snapped inside me.'

'Well,' said the officer, 'that's what your solicitor will call "acting out of character". And then, of course, there are the mitigating circumstances to consider.'

'You mean the fact that Andrew set my studio on fire?'

The policeman shook his head. 'No, I don't mean that at all. I was thinking more of the stress you've been under recently with your father's death.'

Michael blinked in surprise. 'How do you know about that?'

'I've been back to speak to your brother and his wife – Kate, isn't

156

it? A very nice girl, I have to say. She thinks that maybe you've been experiencing a few emotional problems connected with the loss of your father.'

'She didn't say anything about a fish, did she?'

The officer looked at him long and hard. 'The point I'm making,' he said, eventually, 'is that if you're experiencing any kind of major emotional distress in your life, it doesn't necessarily pay to try and hide it. Speak to your solicitor, he may well think it worthwhile to raise the issue in court. Grief affects people in many different ways. The magistrates will take that into account. These things can all be seen as mitigating circumstances.'

'But what about the fire? What about the fact that Andrew –'

'We don't know that, Mr Marshall. He says he doesn't know anything about it, and until we've managed to get hold of the fire brigade's report we've no reason to believe that he does.'

'But –'

'I know, I know, you've already told me. He once went out with your girlfriend, and he once said something vaguely threatening at a party.'

'It's more than that, though. It's ... It's ... '

The officer smiled wearily. 'Look, if we feel that there are any grounds to support your suspicion, then of course we'll delve into it a little deeper. But as things stand ... '

He smiled again, and stood up. 'Now then, I'm going to pop you back in your cell for another twenty minutes or so while we finish off the paperwork and then you'll be free to go. All being well we'll be in touch tomorrow with your court date. Is there anything you need, or anything else you want to ask?'

'No,' said Michael. 'Thank you.'

The officer returned him to his cell. It was a long twenty minutes.

Michael unlocks the door and enters his house. It feels as cold and empty as the police cell. He flicks on the lights, goes into the kitchen, and automatically opens the fridge before he realises that he doesn't want a beer. He puts the kettle on instead, then walks into the lounge and throws himself exhausted onto the sofa.

He lies there and remembers with deep embarrassment the way the kindly officer had looked at him when he'd asked if Kate had said anything about a fish. He must have thought that was some kind of a question. He wishes he could have told the officer about the pike, what it had meant to him. He almost feels that he owed it to the man to tell him the proper truth. Because he knows exactly what it was that made him go berserk, what had turned him, however briefly, into a man of violence. It wasn't Andrew's torching of the studio itself, though that was despicable enough. It wasn't the loss of the specimens that were waiting for sale, or his tools, or his books. It was the loss of his mother, for a second time. But he couldn't tell the constable that, and he won't be able to tell the court, either. Because it's plainly crazy. What kind of person communicates with his dead mother through a stuffed fish, then beats the hell out of someone for destroying it? He closes his eyes tightly, as if to squeeze this heavy question from his mind, and it's two hours later when he wakes up again.

He's confused. It's now eight o'clock at night, and the sky beyond his window is pitch black. He isn't sure at first whether he's looking out at an evening, or a morning. He goes over to his telephone answering machine. The clock on the digital display tells him that it is still the same day, that his sleep was only brief. The display also tells him that he had received some messages in his absence. He doesn't press the button to start running them. Doubtless, well-intentioned words are held there, but there are no words that can take this wretchedness away. It's all such a mess.

And Clare. In two days he'll be going to the airport to meet her off her plane. How's she going to react to all this? As if he doesn't know.

He makes himself a sandwich while the kettle re-boils. He makes a cup of tea and he sits at the kitchen table. He doesn't want to think, about anything. He doesn't want to think about the past, which stretches interminably behind him, riddled with distress. He doesn't want to think of the here and now, this cold house, this numbness of isolation and apathy. He doesn't want to think of the future, a gaping chasm of uncertainty into which he must surely fall. The bread of his sandwich is dry, almost to the point of being stale. He thinks about that, instead.

He turns on the radio and winds the tuning dial with his thumb, searching for something alien and distracting. He stumbles upon a football phone-in, and the words that come from the speaker are immediately repeated in his head. *It was criminal, absolutely criminal. I don't know which game the referee was watching but it wasn't the one I saw. Well that was it, wasn't it, they were demoralised. It was downhill all the way after that.*

43

You have nine new messages.

First new message, received yesterday, at 9.32 a.m:
Hello, this is Alison from N.T.S., just phoning to let you know that the lacquer you ordered will be with you within the next few days. Sorry about the delay. Thanks. Bye.

Second new message, received yesterday, at 11.03 a.m:
Mike, it's Donny. Where are you? I hate these bloody answerphones! Get yourself a mobile!

Third new message, received yesterday, at 11.05 a.m:
If you do decide to get a mobile, I know a bloke who does them dead cheap.

Fourth new message, received yesterday, at 1.46 p.m:
Brrrrrrrrrrrrrrrrrrrrrrrrrrrrrrrrrrrrrrrrrrrrrrrr, kih-kuh.

Fifth new message, received today, at 10.57 a.m:
Michael, it's your Aunt Eileen. I've just heard. Give me a ring when you get back, love, OK? I'll speak to you then. Bye.

Sixth new message, received today, at 11.10 a.m:
Michael, it's Jim, at the sanctuary. We've another badger for you, I'm afraid. Came in last night. We thought we might be able to save him, but … Anyway, if you could call in sooner rather than later. Thanks.

Seventh new message, received today, at 11.54 a.m:
Brrrrrrrrrrrrrrrrrrrrrrrrrrrrrrrrrrrrrrrrrrrrrrrr, kih-kuh.

Eighth new message, received today, at 1.56 p.m:
Mr Marshall, this is Colin Barber, from the regional fire investigation department. I'd like to meet up with you at some point, to tie up a few loose ends regarding the fire in your studio. I have some information that you're going to need for insurance purposes. It appears that the fire was caused by a fault in your heater, but I'll be able to give you the full details when I see you. If you could give me a ring on 02183 211611, during office hours, we can get it all sewn up. Thanks.

Ninth new message, received today, at 2.41 p.m:
Michael, it's Clare. I'm pregnant.

44

Pregnant! Jesus Christ, she's pregnant! That means she's going to have a baby! Only, no, hang on, don't be so stupid. It doesn't mean that at all, does it? It only means she could, perhaps, if she wanted to. Though even then ...

But if she wanted a baby she wouldn't be in Australia seeing about a teaching course. And if she wanted a baby she'd have it with someone who didn't have ridiculous outbursts and beat up ex-boyfriends, and she wouldn't give him the happy news with a couple of terse words on an answerphone.

Tomorrow. She's flying back tomorrow. You're not supposed to fly when you're pregnant. Or maybe that's only in the later stages, I don't know. And what difference does it make, if she doesn't want it?

'It', I'm saying. Just so much material.

Or ...

But I mustn't start that. I mustn't even begin to think that.

And I have, already, because I can't help it. Like when I asked Clare out, I can't not do it. Like it's fated, and it has to happen. Like what I'm seeing is part of some big plan to restore the balance. The intended child dies, the unintended lives. And I know it's just more stupidity but there I am, with a baby cradled in my arms. And there's Clare, the anxious new mother – so tired, but smiling. Clare who wasn't ready for this but wouldn't be without him, not now.

So it's a him, then. A boy.

He'll need his father, won't he?

Boys need their fathers.

45

He goes to meet Clare off her plane, as planned. She walks into the arrivals lounge with her two small suitcases, scanning the area for his face, and it makes his heart leap to see her again. She looks exhausted, and beautiful beyond belief. It feels as if she's been away forever.

Michael waves, catches her attention, and she greets him with a fleeting frown. He trots over to her and offers to carry her cases. Almost reluctantly, she lets him take one of them. He looks into her face, desperate for some further indication of how she is feeling. She gives him nothing.

They are walking out of the lounge when she asks, in little more than a whisper, 'Did you get my message?'

'Yes,' he says. 'Yes, I did.'

'Good. I'm sorry I told you that way, but you weren't there, and I had to let you know. I was in shock. I still am. I don't know how it could have happened, I don't know what went wrong.'

'No.'

She stops in her tracks and turns on him, her eyes flashing. 'Is that all you've got to say? No?'

Michael gasps, stunned by the sudden ferocity of her tone. 'I don't know what else to say. I don't know what you want to hear.'

She drops her case onto the floor and erupts into bitter laughter. 'What I want to hear? Since when did you tell me what I want to hear? You're the man who told me that you were angry with me because I hadn't sat around my whole life waiting for you to appear like some pissed up knight in shining armour. You're the man who can't handle the fact that I happen to have had sex with another man before I met you. Several men, as it happens, but that's hardly the point, is it?' She's shouting now, and a number of travel-weary tourists have stopped in their tracks and are watching the scene with expressions that vary from mild disapproval to barely concealed amusement. 'And now, when I should be looking forward to the rest of my life, I find out that I'm pregnant!'

She puts her hands to her head and bursts into tears. Michael wants to take her in his arms and reassure her, but he can't. She doesn't yet know about the fire, about what he's done to Andrew, about the fact that he spent the morning in court and will be spending two hundred hours of his near future digging old ladies' gardens. It's going to make a difference. Difficult as it is to imagine, things are going to get worse. With this one thought in his mind, Michael stands bowed, rooted in his misery.

Clare composes herself, and snatches up her case again. The watching tourists, sensing that the little drama has peaked, begin to disperse and head off, ready to pick up the threads of their own lives.

'Let's go,' she says, abruptly. 'I need some sleep.'

46

Michael and Kate are standing in the blackened box of the studio, surveying the damage. Not much has survived the fire.

Kate sees something on the floor and she bends down to pick it up. It's a small brass plate. She takes a tissue from her pocket and rubs the soot from the plate and words appear on the dulled surface: *Taxidermy by Michael Marshall, Woodington, England.* She offers it to him, but he doesn't take it.

'Throw it back on the floor,' he says.

She puts it in her pocket.

'Look, Michael, is there anything I can do? Are there clients who need contacting? Or suppliers? I wouldn't mind, you know.'

'No. Thanks, but I can sort all that out myself.'

'What about your insurance company, have you phoned them?'

'Yes,' he says. 'Like I said, I can sort it. It's ... '

'What?'

'It's not that I need help with.'

She pauses. 'I know.'

His voice cracks. 'I haven't seen her for days, Kate. She won't answer my calls. I don't know whether or not I should go round. I want to, but I'm scared. I've made such a mess of everything.'

Kate sighs. 'My advice,' she says, slowly, 'would be to give her some space. Give her some time to think things over. And don't ... ' She sighs again, more heavily this time.

'What?'

'Don't expect anything too unlikely.'

'You mean don't expect her to have the baby?'

'Yes.'

'But –'

'You've got to see this from her point of view, Michael. She's young, she'll have plans. And I dare say these last few months – and don't forget it's only been a few months – haven't been easy for her, either.'

'I know that, but I can't help thinking –'

'Thinking does no good at a time like this,' she says, trying to inject some positivity into the conversation. 'Action, that's what you need. Something to stop you dwelling on things.'

'Well there's always my community service. That starts in a couple of weeks.'

'I was thinking more along the lines of you getting your business back together.'

He gives her a small, forlorn smile. 'I don't know.'

'What do you mean?'

'It doesn't seem important any more.'

'Michael, it's your life!'

He laughs, bitterly. 'And what kind of a life? It's not real, is it? Nothing I do is real.'

She reaches out and touches him on his shoulder. 'Michael, calm down. The world is not about to end. You have years ahead of you.'

'Years of what, though, Kate? Years of waiting for something that will never happen again? Years of regret, because I screwed up my one chance of happiness?'

'Michael, it wasn't your fault.'

'What difference does that make? How does that help? I could have been happy, I could have made her happy. I could have been a ... And I could have done it properly, don't you see? I could have done it properly.'

47

The old Woodington Secondary School, an imposing Victorian building long since converted into a library and leisure centre, stands off High Street, just up from the Market Place. The exterior of the building has been little changed over the years and it still retains its twin front doors, one for the boys, and one for the girls. The stumps of the railings that in Victorian times split the playground in two lie somewhere beneath the tarmac of what is now the town's main car park.

Next to the school there is a tiny stone-built Methodist chapel, and next to that a modest motor garage with four bulky petrol pumps crowding its small forecourt. Between the chapel and the garage is the entrance to a narrow alley, known as The Jitty, which goes on to connect with Penn Lane. The Jitty signals the start of a public footpath to Wenleigh. A wooden stile on the opposite side of Penn Lane allows the journey to continue through Brown's Fields and down into the remnants of the valley. Michael, as one of the last pupils to have attended the secondary school, walked this journey a thousand times.

The Jitty passes along the edge of four abandoned tennis courts, which lie on a square of ground that meets the rear of the garage at one end, and the garden walls of two of Penn Lane's large country houses at the other. The tennis courts belonged, until recently, to the wealthy owner of Woodington's shoe factory which, after years of resisting the inevitable, finally closed six months ago, another casualty of cheap imported goods. The owner, deciding to leave for pastures new, donated the ground to Woodington's town council as a parting gift. Now, the tennis courts are to be converted into a leisure area and playground. Michael, as part of his community service, is helping with the initial stages of this transformation.

Michael was given the choice between getting his punishment out of the way in a solid block, or spreading it out over a sustained period of time. He chose to do it this way, working for five weeks, at forty hours a week. This way, his near future is neatly taken care of. He can work all day, and drink all night.

Yesterday, when he began, the man from the probation service had stayed with him, explaining what was to be done, and satisfying himself that Michael was up to the job. This morning he appeared only briefly, to check that the skip firm had delivered the skips as promised, and that Michael had turned up. Now Michael is alone.

The work is not complicated. He has to remove weeds, loosen rubble, dig trenches, dismantle broken fences. What is harder than the work is the steady stream of walkers who throw inquisitive looks in his direction as they make their way along The Jitty. Some of them, despite Michael's best efforts not to make eye contact, insist on stopping for a chat. They speak to him in optimistic tones through the wire fencing, like people visiting a prisoner. Most of them mean well. They are glad to see the land finally being put to good use. Some of the older ones even thank him, as if the whole thing had been his idea.

Michael is now standing in a corner of the plot, looking at a small forest of dead nettles. The nettles make him think of his own garden, and then of Clare. He shakes his head, he mustn't think of her. He's still heard nothing from her, and he's sure in his heart that it's over. He plunges himself into the nettles, tearing them up from the ground and throwing them past his shoulders.

He gathers the nettles together and makes a fire. The flames rip through them with a startling ferocity. He thinks of his studio burning, of his books, his journals, his tools, all destroyed. He hasn't yet made any effort to get the studio refitted. He still doesn't know if he's going to. There no longer seems any point, to anything.

Last night, Kate called to see him. He was hopelessly drunk. She wanted to know why he hadn't been round for his tea for the last few Saturdays. She said he should. She said he must come this week. She said everything would be all right, in time, he'll see. She was wrong. Nothing will be all right, ever. It never has been, and it never will be.

He's given up with Phil. Sooner or later, he knows, Phil will come ambling awkwardly down The Jitty with Gypsy in tow, and the two of them will be once more obliged to make some stupid embarrassing small talk. But where's the surprise in that? Why should they be able to talk to each other? They are just two men, after all, two very different men. It's unfathomable, the fact that they shared the same mother.

The same mother; the mother that Michael no longer has. Not just because of the pike, but because he has finally evicted that little boy who held on to her for so long. He has dragged him screaming from out of the depths of himself, and has cast him aside forever. The mistakes he made with Clare, mistakes he will pay for always, were down to that little boy. The trauma he underwent with his father's death, and all the needless anguish he put the old man through, was down to that selfish, self-obsessed little boy.

Three months down the line, Michael finds it hard to believe that he could have been so cruel to his father, so unforgiving. He keeps thinking about the funeral, about all those people packed into the church, about the enthusiasm they had put into their singing of the hymns. Those people weren't praising some higher entity, he knows that. It wasn't about God, that beautiful sound, whatever the minister might have wanted to believe. It was about Dennis. And although Michael still doesn't know who half of those people in the church were, he now knows why they were there. They were there because they had a deeply held respect for his father. They can't have known him any more than Michael did, but they knew him well enough to step outside of their own lives for a day, to celebrate his life, and to mourn his passing. They must have seen in him some essential unspoken decency.

As Michael rakes down the ashes from the nettle fire, images of his father fill his head. He sees him in the hospital bed, broken and defeated. He sees him, awkward and embarrassed, holding up an oak leaf and asking for glue. He sees him standing in front of the farmhouse, gazing intently up at the reservoir wall. As if trying to see beyond it. As if trying to take himself back to a better time, lost beneath all that water.

Because the bird box was already on the wall when Michael bought the house, he has no idea how it is fixed. Presumably, there will be brackets of some sort on the back. He unfolds his set of step ladders, climbs them, and takes a look. The gap between the back of the box and the wall is tight, and it's difficult to see.

He readjusts his balance. The slabs beneath him are still icy from last night's frost, and he's worried that the steps might flip out sideways when he starts to push. When he's satisfied that they won't, he leans over, grips the box with both hands, and begins. At first, it looks as if the box is stuck fast, and will break before it will move. Its thin walls distort and bow with the pressure of Michael's hands, but then it suddenly slides upwards and comes free.

There are, as Michael had thought, two metal plates fastened to the wall, with corresponding, and equally corroded, brackets on the back of the box. He brings the box to his chest, climbs back down, and sits on his back doorstep to study it further. The roof, which was already deteriorating badly when the hornet queen had first decided to make her home there, is now severely buckled and splayed. Without effort, Michael is able to peel off, one after another, the unglued slices of the plywood, like so many layers of skin. Only the very bottom layers of the ply remain sound, their joint thickness just enough for them still to cling to the rusty nails pinning them to the box's sides.

Taking his penknife from his pocket, Michael levers off what remains of the roof. It comes away with the crown of the hornets' nest still attached to it, so that he is left looking into the nest's swirling inner landscape. He gently probes it with his finger, the fine papery material crumbling to dust as he does so, like beige-coloured ash. Working his finger deeper into the nest, he comes against something solid – the top layer of the cells in which the young were raised. He moves his hand around in a circular motion, loosening the fabric around the hard shape of the ball of cells, then lifts it out like a prize. Tiny flakes of the crumbled wood-paper fall around him like confetti, and three dead hornets drop onto his lap. He puts the cell structure down, picks up one of the hornets by its wing, and raises it in front of his face. It's only then that he sees Clare, standing a few feet away, watching him.

'Your gate was open. I ... '

Michael lowers his eyes and gently places the hornet on the ground beside him. He doesn't speak.

'What are you doing?' asks Clare.

He gestures towards the bird box. 'I was cleaning it out.' He wants to get up and put his arms around her, but he daren't move.

'Are you hoping one of the queens will come back next year?'

'No, the chances of that are tiny. I don't know why I'm doing it, to be honest.'

'Oh.'

He glances up at her. 'I was thinking about all the work. All the work that went into that nest, just for one season.'

'But all things are relative, aren't they?' she says. 'I imagine six months is a long time for a hornet.'

'It can be a long time for us humans, too.'

'I know it can.'

He finally looks into her face. 'Why are you here, Clare?'

She hesitates. 'I'm not really sure. But I'm sorry I've been avoiding you. Perhaps that's why I've come, to say that.'

'I see,' says Michael.

She sighs, exasperated with herself. 'No, that's not it,' she says. 'I've been doing a lot of thinking. About what I want, and what I don't want. And I've been doing a lot of talking, mostly to Jaz.'

172

Michael takes his eyes off her and gazes down at the burnt-out shell of the studio. 'I don't imagine she has anything good to say about me, after what I did to her brother.'

'You'd be surprised,' says Clare.

'I didn't mean to hit him, you know. I've never hit anyone before. Something inside me just ... I was so sure it was him who had started the fire.' His eyes linger on the remains of his studio, his first real studio, the reason he bought this house in the first place. When he returns his attention to Clare, she's crouching in front of him.

'I wouldn't worry too much about Andrew,' she says. 'I went to see him the other day, and apart from reinforcing his opinion of you I don't think you did any lasting damage.'

'Good.'

'And anyway, it's not his opinion of you that matters. It's mine.'

He tries to read the look in her eyes, but he can't. 'And what is your opinion of me?'

'I don't know, Michael, that's the problem. But then again, I hardly know what to make of myself these days.' There's a moment's silence, then she says softly: 'What I think I'd like is for us to talk. Properly. Can we do that?'

'Yes,' he says. 'Yes, we can.'

'And you understand that's all I want, that I'm not promising anything?'

'Yes.'

She smiles. 'Good. Then can we continue this conversation indoors, please, because it's freezing out here.'

'Oh yes,' he says.

And they go inside, to start the talking.

∾

A Note About the Author

Gregory Heath was born in Melbourne, Derbyshire, in 1967, and has an MA in Narrative Writing. He has taught Writing, Psychology, Literature and Film in a variety of settings, and currently runs an Access to HE programme at an FE college. He is widely published in the small press, his poetry, short stories and essays having appeared in magazines such as *Tears in the Fence*, *Iota*, and *Poetic Licence*. *Staple* have published him on a number of occasions and recently featured him in their *Alt-gen* collection showcasing the best small press writers of the last decade.

OTHER BOOKS FROM

WAYWISER

POETRY

Al Alvarez, *New & Selected Poems*

Peter Dale, *One Another*

B.H. Fairchild, *The Art of the Lathe*

Jeffrey Harrison, *The Names of Things: New & Selected Poems*

Joseph Harrison, *Someone Else's Name*

Anthony Hecht, *Collected Later Poems*

Anthony Hecht, *The Darkness and the Light*

Eric McHenry, *Potscrubber Lullabies*

Timothy Murphy, *Very Far North*

Ian Parks, *Shell Island*

Daniel Rifenburgh, *Advent*

Mark Strand, *Blizzard of One**

Deborah Warren, *The Size of Happiness*

Clive Watkins, *Jigsaw*

Richard Wilbur, *Mayflies**

Richard Wilbur, *Collected Poems 1943-2004*

Norman Williams, *One Unblinking Eye*

FICTION

Matthew Yorke, *Chancing It*

NON-FICTION

Neil Berry, *Articles of Faith: The Story of British Intellectual Journalism*

Mark Ford, *A Driftwood Altar: Essays and Reviews*

Richard Wollheim, *Germs: A Memoir of Childhood*

*Expanded UK edition